W9-CII-346

HIBISCUS
MASK

Rich Shapero

HIBISCUS MASK

a novel

HALF MOON BAY, CALIFORNIA

TooFar Media
500 Stone Pine Road, Box 3169
Half Moon Bay, CA 94019

© 2024 by Rich Shapero

All Rights Reserved.

No part of this book may be reproduced or transmitted in any form
or by any means, electronic or mechanical, including photocopying,
recording, or by any information storage and retrieval system, without
permission in writing from the publisher.

This is a book of fiction, and none of the characters are intended to
portray real people. Names, characters, places and incidents are either
the products of the author's imagination or are used fictitiously.

Library of Congress Cataloging-in-Publication Data is available.

ISBN: 978-1-7335259-9-2

Cover collage and design by Michael Baron Shaw, with Eugene Von
Bruenchenhein (EVB 380, 1955; EVB 385, 1956); "Elegant Girl" by
Egor Mayer; "Portrait of a Woman" by angel_nt.
Artwork copyright © 2024, 2009, 2008 Rich Shapero

Printed in the United States of America

27 26 25 24   1 2 3 4 5

Also by Rich Shapero
Beneath Caaqi's Wings
Dreams of Delphine
The Slide That Buried Rightful
Dissolve
Island Fruit Remedy
Balcony of Fog
Rin, Tongue and Dorner
Arms from the Sea
The Hope We Seek
Too Far
Wild Animus

1

*B*ehind, a motorbike threatens, grind ascending, forcing Kell aside. It's Chulia Street, a wet night with no sidewalk. He's on the asphalt behind a mother and stroller. To the left, lit cafes and flaming grills, hawkers stirring laksa and waving ladles. On the corner, ball-capped tourists and headscarfed locals, umbrellas in hand, folded but ready for rain. In a couple of hours, the street girls would appear with their penciled brows, padded bras, narrowed eyes and sly smiles.

Kell turns, enters Love Lane, hopping puddles, hearing stray whistles and shouts as he crosses the frozen traffic beneath a trapeze of lights, headed toward one of the neon eateries. An American—collared shirt, sand-colored pants, an exemplar of science adrift, lost in a foreign land. Lonely and lost. Threatened by age, forty-two, and a clashing heritage. His black curls and stern jaw came from an Irish father, but the fire of Sicilia burns in his heart, a disharmony barely noticed in the Asian land.

Lonely but aware in a way few locals are: Kell understands the equatorial jungle. And the jungle is everywhere, crowding Penang's largest city, surrounding towns, swallowing homes, woven into the lives of the people.

A bar hustler calls, stepping forward, motioning. Kell waves him away.

He knows the horde, plants and pollinators, birds and bugs, leeches and charmers, monsters and freaks. A botanist, an intellectual, he is nonetheless shrewd. He understands life as a struggle and expects conflict; and this, along with an inborn agility, keeps him safe. But being a man without a woman— That's not the life he'd imagined. He has no desire to count years without love, but what he wants he hasn't found.

He ducks under the awning of a corner cafe, scanning those seated out front and standing around the bar. A thin woman, swarthy, likely Indian, is fixed on him, raising her hand, moving from behind a table. Not the woman he's looking for.

"Mr. Kell?" She touches her fingers to her heart.

Kell stops, stares, nods once, unsure.

"Nitti asked me to meet you," the thin woman says. "She's waiting at a club a few minutes away. My name is Yrine."

An intermediary? He was expecting a woman named Nitti. They'd found each other on a dating app and agreed to this time and place the week before.

"I live here, in Georgetown," Yrine says. She has black

pearl earrings and her nose is sharp. Her eyes read his concern. She motions, starting between the tables. "She's at the Qing Club. Will you come with me?"

He's rooted for a moment, wondering. Is Yrine some kind of chaperon? In her procedurality, it seems some custom is being honored. After two years in the country, he is still confused by things like this. Kell ignores the uncertainty and follows.

Women who are willing to consider a non-Muslim are in the minority here, but during his stay he's met quite a few. His mind has been often engaged, his heart almost never. With her, however— With Nitti, his expectations are higher. From the video she'd posted and from their phone conversations, he'd gotten a sense of her gravity and depth. She was more thoughtful than most. She wasn't looking for entertainment or a night of good humor, and that's fired his hopes. Intensity, depth of feeling, a desire for real understanding—

"She's eager to meet you," Yrine says.

The Indian woman speaks excellent English as many here do.

"But she's nervous," Yrine adds with a smile.

Everyone's nervous meeting a stranger, he thinks.

He follows Yrine over a five-foot rain gutter and across Chulia, then down a side street with hawker carts like pandanus thickets crowding a shore. They'd been pedaled into place early that day, and they'd vanish when the last of the girls had gone.

"It's a bit hard to find," Yrine says.

Kell recalls the phone interactions, the pics and the video he watched. Nitti's voice is small, high-pitched but lofty: the

3

kwee-kwee of a serpent-eagle circling in the clouds. Lips full, skin coppery, nose bowed like the bud of a bamboo orchid; hair black and iridescent as a drongo's tail. Nitti is a beautiful woman.

"She's a rare creature," Yrine says, as if she could hear his thoughts.

Kell is walking beside her now. Smoke rises from a hawker grill, carrying odors of curry and scorched shrimp. A hunch-backed woman stoops over a wok.

Mingled with Nitti's gravity was a playfulness and irony like his own. It is hard to stifle his hopes. He wants it all: kinship, purity, heart in hand; a life together, weighty but keen. In advance of a first encounter, he's had thoughts like this before. It was all just ignorant desire. Was Yrine going to join them?

"You work at the Botanical Gardens," she says.

He nods. "I'm creating gingers. And you?"

"I manage the desk at a small hotel near the Hin Depot."

They are past the hawkers now. The street here is dark, warehouses looming on either side. Beneath a balcony in a ring of motorbikes, rempit punks sit like macaques, smoking, yawning to show their fangs as the two pass.

Yrine veers toward a leaning warehouse, slows, looks into a barred window and opens a black door. A red wall appears, painted with ideograms. She crosses the threshold, turns right, draws back a scarlet drape and enters a vestibule. Wooden birdcages hang from the ceiling, wound with tinsel.

She stops and faces him. "Can I see your passport please?"

4

Kell stares at her.

"There are men who prey on women like Nitti," Yrine explains. "I need to make sure you are who you say you are."

Kell is speechless.

"She's driven an hour and a half to see you," Yrine says.

He sighs, removes his passport from his pocket and hands it over. Odd moments were a part of romance in a foreign land. There were always surprises.

After inspecting his passport, Yrine returns it to him with a smile and continues forward. He follows her across the vestibule, ducks beneath an arch and steps into a long room lit by flashing red lights and red paper lanterns. Around a stage at the room's center, small groups and couples huddle at low tables, eating, drinking, adding murmurs to a fog of Asian music.

Yrine leads him past the stage. A giant serpent with a dragon's head is poised over it, jaws gaping. In a dim alcove, a woman is seated at a high-top table, turned half away. Her bare neck and shoulders are visible, along with a red hibiscus pinned to a black coif, braided and bound up with meticulous care.

The hibiscus is a splash, like fruit thrown at a wall. Its petals are flounced and the anther is gone. The woman's arms are gently muscled. Her skin looks burnished, smooth as a costly fabric. As they approach the table, Kell can see the hibiscus edges have creped. Removed from the stalk, it has started to wilt.

The woman turns. For a moment the light from a rotating

strobe obscures her face, then Yrine takes the seat at her elbow, Kell moves to a vacant chair, and enough shadow returns to Nitti's features to see them clearly.

The bowed nose, the high brow; gentle cheeks, coppery and poreless. And her eyes—forlorn, startling eyes—dark and deep and pointed with light. They track him as he seats himself. Cautious, polite but private, evaluating.

"He's tall, isn't he," Yrine says.

Nitti seems not to hear.

Kell tips his head. "Thank you for making the trip."

A fragrance reaches him—sweet, exotic, like steeped clitoria.

"I had a feeling," Nitti says softly.

Then her gaze—guarded but daring—ventures forward, approaching with the foggy music, crossing the space between them. The rapport they'd struck during their conversations had been no illusion.

"I wasn't listening," she apologizes. "What did you say?"

"I thanked you for making the trip."

"You've come the longer distance," she says. "You're far from home."

"I'm a water gentian. The stem broke and I floated away, thinking I might take root somewhere else."

"A fine explanation." She laughs at his words—lightly, poking fun.

"I'm here because of the jungle," he says.

"Your profession," she nods. "I'm intrigued by that."

There's an invitation in the dark eyes.

"The jungle is us," he says. "Our real nature."

"Us?"

"Threat and attraction. The fight to survive. Things that don't matter are swept away." He's trying to touch that depth, the authenticity lurking beneath her flawless composure.

"You change the genes of plants," she says.

"For me," he nods, "that's exciting: feeling a breath of the creativity that fashioned our world."

"How God might feel," Nitti says.

"Or an artist," he says. "I painted with my fingers when I was a child."

With these words, he gives access to an élan from his youth, waving his hand, diluting his earnestness with a smiling naïveté, surrendering adult aspirations to the triumph of simple curiosity.

She responds to his buoyancy and the wonder in his eyes as if it's a lucky gift. Her smile, Kell sees, is raw and authentic; and in its ripening is an assumption about the inherent generosity of life. Her face shifts forward, her shoulders relax.

A silent moment. A moment of understanding. You don't have to be on guard with me, Kell thinks. The defenses are gone now. When they spoke, they would be talking like old friends, in a simpler language, unselfconscious, like people who have known each other all their lives.

And then, in a heartbeat, Kell sees a chasm open between them.

Nitti draws back. In response to some hidden emotion, her dark eyes harden. Has something surprised or disturbed her?

"You're staring at me," he says.

"I'm sorry. I have to go."

Kell feels an electric chill in his chest. "What's wrong?"

He looks at Yrine, and she's as surprised as he is.

Nitti rises from her chair, turning her head, hiding her face. She's stepping away from the table.

Why is she fleeing? Kell leaves his seat.

She's moving quickly now, passing the stage and the dragon's head, and he's hurrying after her. *Blind instinct*, a rational voice objects. But Kell doesn't care. Nitti's a white morph of the paradise flycatcher. You might see her once, but you could look for the rest of your life and never see her again.

He catches up to her as she enters the vestibule.

Speaking her name, he grabs hold of her arm.

She halts, stiff and quivering, not fighting him off, burying her feelings.

"Where are you going?" he says.

She shakes her head.

Beneath the birdcages, against the wall, there's a bench and a stool.

"Please," Kell says, gesturing toward them.

She eyes him for a long moment. Then she sighs and sits. Kell descends with her.

"What happened?" he asks.

"You reminded me of someone."

"Someone who hurt you," he says.

She seals her lids, still upset by the recognition.

"No," she sighs. "It wasn't like that."

8

"Are you afraid of me?"

A laugh beneath her breath. "I suppose I am." Her tone now is self-accusing, as if disclosing the truth might shame her or unveil something unworthy.

"Fear is love's enemy," Kell says.

"That's a child speaking."

He can't tell if her words are critical or accepting.

"Is a child listening?" he asks.

She seems to mull the question, agitated but tempted, weighing the risks of answering.

"Perhaps," she says finally, drawing a breath. Her eyes meet his—warily, cautiously. "Is that what you're looking for?"

"It is," Kell says.

The sound of a wooden flute reaches them, moody, mystical.

"I'm not a child," Nitti says.

Speaking to her, he thinks, is like a jungle trek. The screen of green admits your vision at every angle. With every step, you're drawn into its unseen depths.

"You've been married," she says.

"I have."

"What happened?"

"It was a miracle while it lasted."

"There have been other women since, no doubt."

He nods. "Wonderful women."

"Don't entertain me, Mr. Kell."

He laughs. "And some not so wonderful." Then more seriously, "You can be friendly."

Nitti exhales. She closes her eyes and leans her head to one side. Then she reaches toward him, opening her fist.

Kell looks at the delicate palm and the narrow fingers.

"I'm sorry," she says.

He clasps her hand, feeling its warmth and the curl of her digits.

"You left your country," Kell says. "Like I did."

"That was years ago."

"Boston is halfway around the world," he says. "What made you do that? Set down so far from home." It seemed like a simple question.

"You're making me nervous." She opens her eyes and looks away.

"I don't mean to."

Nitti is shaking her head. She takes a breath as if about to speak, then stops herself. Kell can feel her power, fierce but precarious. She's like a leaning putat at the river's edge, trunk still growing. How long could she hold the pose before her roots gave out?

"You're the one I've been—"

"You don't know," she says. She pulls her hand from his and settles it in her lap, edgy as a mimosa now, leaves folding up. Between them, a vacuum of feeling opens. She's made a quiet decision, he sees.

She straightens herself, calmer, resolved. There's a kind of nobility in her resignation, as if she is choosing the moral path, doing what's best for them both.

Her brows arch and her eyes meet his. "I'm attracted to

you, Mr. Kell. But this isn't going to work."

Nitti rises without looking at him and heads for the outside door.

The next moment, Yrine steps into the birdcage room. She looks puzzled.

Only then does Kell realize that the doors of all the cages are open.

There was no forgetting her. Days passed, but his fixation didn't abate. Other women lived on the surface of things. Nitti was somehow in touch with the core. Kell imagined he could feel her desire—her need—along with the void of confidence and trust. He called three hotels near the Hin Depot. Yrine was a desk clerk at the third. She didn't respond to his first call or his second. When he stopped by it was her day off. But on Monday of the following week, she showed up at the Ginger House.

He's in the open-air enclosure, walls of green wire mesh around him, sun shining on his brow and front. Kell raises a small potted plant, touching its stalk, pleased with its strength. He pinches a withered leaf and removes it, then checks the dampness of the soil with his middle finger. His cellphone chimes.

He replaces the pot on the trestle with dozens of others and exits the pen, seeing Yrine ascending the path with one of the Botanical Gardens' staff.

Kell waves to her and steps forward, touching his fingers to his heart.

"Thanks for coming," he says.

"I doubt I'm going to be any help," she replies. "It's been years," Yrine sighs, looking around.

The high wall of the jungle rises from the Gardens' border, scored by a hanging cascade and bottomed by nibung palms.

"The Fragrance Atrium is new," he says, "and so is the Orchid House. The aviary and animal pens went up five years ago. When were you here?"

"I was a teenager," Yrine replies. "It was only flowers and forest then." She recalls, "You were flooded last August."

"We were," Kell says. A typhoon as fierce as a dozen monsoons had drowned the Gardens. He points to a raw face on the canyon wall. "A peak came away." He swings his arm. "This turned into a lake. Monitors got through the fences." The eight-foot reptiles were like dinosaurs descending the slopes. "They were swimming here, around the enclosure and in the shed. When the sun came out, they climbed onto the roof to relax. One of the females left eggs in the pantry."

He motions her to follow him, leading the way up the path. Through the enclosure entrance, over coiled hoses, beside the seedbeds and trestles crowded with plants.

"Our creations," Kell says, scanning the growths. "Your country is ginger's gene pool. Did you know that? A hundred and fifty species, more or less."

"And the purpose?" she asks.

"We're looking for new gingerols—oils produced and

stored in the roots. To treat disease." He leads her down an aisle through more mature plants. "Gingerol affects the production of insulin, prevents the formation of blood clots. It can be used as a febrifuge, a diuretic or a purgative." Kell stops before a chest-high growth. "Pharma pays the bills. I'm not driven by altruism," he admits. "I like playing with plants."

"This one's attractive," Yrine says.

The inflorescence is a spike of amber shells.

"An alpinia," Kell says. "Smell." He raises a shell to her nose.

"Like cardamom," she says.

"It doesn't exist in the wild. We made it here, using foreign genes."

He turns and touches the leaves of a costus ginger. "Our power to change them has limits. Some plants have qualities we can't edit out."

"You're going to stay here?" Yrine asks.

"I have no plans to leave," Kell says. "Penang's a good place for me. One of the oldest rainforests in the world, and I don't have to live in the jungle to make use of its genetic material. Can we talk about Nitti?"

Before she is able to answer, thunder booms down and rain right behind. It is four and things will be wet for a while. Kell motions, leading her through the enclosure into the office, where he stops beside a desk with a printer and piles of documents. Through an open door, the lab is visible with its incubation cabinets and instruments arrayed on counters. A woman in a white coat is opening a freezer door and removing a frosted tray.

"I want to see her again," Kell says.

"That's not going to happen," Yrine replies.

"Why not?"

"Nitti's an unusual woman," Yrine says.

"She said I reminded her of someone. Do you know who that was?"

Yrine shook her head. "I don't think it matters. Getting close to Nitti can be difficult. Nothing comes easily with her. Ask her a question, you won't get a simple answer; you may not get an answer at all. Her shifts in mood, unexpected retreats, sudden advances— Things must be inferred. Parts of Nitti are hidden."

"Have you spoken to her," he asks, "about that night? About me?"

"I have." Yrine gave him a discouraging look. "She's not what you're looking for."

"What happened in the Qing Club?"

"I don't know," Yrine shook her head. "She had a strong reaction to you. I'm not sure why. But she doesn't want to see you again—of that I'm sure."

"How long have you known her?" he asks.

"We were childhood friends," Yrine says. "We lost touch after she left for the States. Last year we found each other again." Her brow creases, her delivery slows. "Back then," she says, "the family had money. Now, Nitti's father is unemployed. He's a well-meaning man who loves his daughter. But—" Yrine lifts her chin and eyes him gravely. "Like others," she says, "in similar circumstances, he is forced to depend on an attractive daughter and the attentions of men to keep things going."

At this, Kell falters.

"What are you saying?" He shakes his head.

Yrine holds his gaze, sharing her pity, her regret and compassion.

For Kell, it's a waterlogged sun rising over a black swamp.

"She's a prostitute," he says.

Yrine recoils. "It's a terrible unkindness to use that word."

"What else would you call it?"

"Nitti's relationships with men are 'arrangements.' There's affection, support, companionship. It's not about sex. Some don't even involve that. The money is viewed as a gift to the family."

She reads his skepticism and that provokes her.

"It's a committed connection," Yrine says. "An exclusive one. She's faithful, and the man must be too."

"How long has she been doing this?" Kell asks.

"You're not in America," Yrine says, ignoring his question. "Romance isn't everything. Marriages are still planned by parents here. The ability to provide for a woman matters."

Her look turned glum. "For poor Nitti," she mutters, "it's an impossible situation. Her grandfather was a rubber merchant. He had money before the war. That paid for her home and the schools in America. But the rubber trade died and the money ran out. By the time she returned, her grandfather was dead, her mother was ill and her father was jobless. He's past the age of employment now."

"I was a prospective 'arrangement,'" Kell says.

Yrine sighs. "She knew right away you wouldn't be interested in something like that."

The rain is rattling on the metal roof.

"What if I was," Kell says.

His words surprise her. Yrine frowns. "I'm not sure."

She's a rare creature, he thinks. What was the risk?

Kell lives in a small house in Jelutong, ten minutes from Georgetown to the north and ten from Gelugor to the south, the site of University of Science, Malaysia, where he keeps an office.

Many of the country's locales were named after growing things. The jelutong tree could reach fifty meters; its heartwood was white and its grain was straight, but it was soft and prone to insect attack. The place he rents is on a quiet street with jungle nearby, green hills visible through the bedroom windows.

Two days after their meeting at the Gardens, Yrine arrives at his house before dinner. Susilo, Nitti's father, has determined the size of the gift. Kell places the appropriate amount in an envelope, which Yrine delivers. Three days after that, Kell returns from work in the late afternoon and dresses for the visit.

It's an hour and a half from Jelutong to Ipoh. He takes the southern bridge, crossing the water from Penang to the mainland. Beyond the welcoming arch and toll plaza the way is level, transmission towers and palm plantations on either side. South of Taiping, the road cuts through mountains rocky and green with forests steep and dense. He speeds through Kuala Kangsar and descends into the Kinta Valley, a wild aisle bounded by cliffed humps and limestone knobs.

It isn't yet sundown, but the sky is roofed and the air has dimmed. The knobs rise toward the veil of clouds like playthings dropped by a giant, clawed walls and grown-over crags, battered scarps shadowed and silhouetted. As he enters Ipoh, the monoliths loom over stores, body shops and roadside homes.

The address Yrine has given him is at the edge of town, in a woodland that verges a winding river. Kell follows a narrow roadway, spots the number painted on a board, and turns onto an unpaved drive. He eases his car across a weedy apron and switches the motor off. The house is good-sized, on ten-foot stilts, paneled with coffee-colored wood and trimmed in black, with a gray tile roof. A large octagonal room projects in front, with stairs rising to it on either side, a sign of prestige in an earlier time.

He opens the car door and steps out. The stilts are peeling and the ground needs raking. As he crosses the apron, the wistful call of a malkoha reaches him. Dusk is settling, but the air is warm.

The vanes of one of the octagon's shutters shift. Someone is eyeing him through the louvers. Then the shutter opens and the face of a gray-haired woman appears. She fixes on him, pinches her lips with what might be disapproval and motions him toward the stair on the left.

Kell reaches the stair and starts up, grasping a stilt. They protected houses from floods. These were four-sided so snakes couldn't climb them. At the stair's top is a door carved with Islamic stars. Before Kell can knock, it swings back.

The elderly woman faces him—broad nose, thin lips, haggard and dun. Her gnarled hand twitches him across the threshold. The octagon is a guest room, he sees. The woman leads him to a low table surrounded by chairs.

A decanter of tea stands on a silver tray circled by cups. The woman halts behind one of the chairs and nods to him. Kell sits and she departs. A few moments later an old man limps through an archway supporting himself with a cane.

His beige linen suit hangs loosely. His hair is combed straight back, and through the silver threads, his scalp is visible. The hitching gait and fighting eyes give an impression of obstinance and frailty.

"I'm Susilo," the old man says, "Nitti's ayah. Welcome to our *ruang tamu*." He raises his brows. "Shall we have some tea?"

He takes the chair beside Kell, reaches for the decanter and pours the cinnamon liquid into two cups. As Kell watches, his discomfort mounts. Acting casual would be difficult. Whatever the causes, this man had put his daughter in a terrible position.

"You're a scientist, I'm told," Susilo says. "A student of our jungle."

His wording is good, but his diction is wobbly.

"There's no place on earth like it," Kell says.

Susilo smiles. "A man respects what he loves."

Kell recognizes the reach of his words, but he does his best to accept them as a compliment. Don't be too quick to judge him, he tells himself. It would be easy to condemn the man.

"You father new plants," Susilo says.

"Gingers," Kell nods. He gives an example of his genetic forays.

Playing the good host in his guest room is something the old man seems glad to do.

"The science is still in its infancy," Kell says. "My little group knows as much about ginger genetics as any team in the world."

As he speaks, smoke coils from an incense pot on a window sill. Kell knows the wood by its fragrance. Aquilaria is used as a disinfectant. In a dwelling like this, by a river, humidity is high. Fungus and fern spores fill the air.

Susilo plants his cane between his thighs, setting his hands on the ivory knob. "How long will you stay in Penang?"

"I have no plans to leave," Kell says.

Was the old man partial to a longer stay, imagining future payments? Or would a longer stay trouble him? Did he have reasons to fear a more serious attachment?

Susilo is sad-eyed. "She's my only child," he says softly.

Nitti enters the room with her face averted, brisk but casual, in a mango blouse and white slacks. She approaches the chair beside her father, bows her head and seats herself.

Polished, concealing—an enamel box with its lid closed. Kell reminds himself that the discussions about the arrangement had been with Yrine. She had assured him that Nitti would be pleased to know him better. Sitting across from her now, he wonders.

"I was drawn to your daughter," Kell faces Susilo, "instinctively."

The old man turns away.

Kell meant to allay his fears, to share the depth of his feeling, but Susilo doesn't want to know. How is Nitti taking this? She seems calm and unruffled, legs folded to the side, hands in her lap. Her brow tips, the piercing eyes pointing down. She's been through this before, Kell thinks, imagining how the burden must have grown heavier over the years.

"You may break off the arrangement whenever you like," Susilo says. "But as long as it lasts, you must remain faithful to my daughter. Her health depends on that."

"I understand," Kell nods.

"You're a professional man," Susilo says. "I will expect you to act professionally. Nitti is a special woman. She must feel safe with you, protected by you. Do I have your word on that?"

"You do," Kell replies.

The old man faces his daughter, fisting the knob of his cane. His eyes are stern, and so is his unspoken message: don't be accommodating, don't be in a hurry to please; don't show this man too much of yourself too quickly. Nitti takes it all in without a whisper of agitation.

Susilo sighs and leans back in his chair.

"You're a fortunate man," he says, growing cordial again, as if Kell is now part of the family. Kell feels relief and more than a little sympathy. He understands the old man's concern, and his formality has taken some of the sting out of the venal aspect of the match.

"You have your appointment," Susilo asks Nitti.

"Tomorrow morning," she replies.

Susilo smiles at Kell, takes the cane from between his knees and rises. "I'll wish the two of you good evening." He bows to Kell and limps away, crossing the patterned rug quietly.

Nitti rises, extending her hand. "May I show you our ser-ambi?"

Kell rises with her. Her hand is light, airy and warm. The woman who'd shown so much agitation at the Qing Club—puzzling, unexplainable agitation—now seems entirely self-possessed.

She leads him down a corridor. Following closely, Kell catches a sachet of nutmeg and clove, a scent from the under-sides of dark leaves. They released their fragrance when you crushed them. It was desire for spices like these that had led to the region's colonization. Nitti's father was old enough to remember English rule.

She opens a door and they step out onto a veranda facing the river.

Shadows, twilight. The loud ringing of cicadas sug-gests a storm. On the river's near side: fan palms, drooping mengkuang, rock speckled with lichen, and a narrow path fol-lowing the water. On the far side, the jungle climbs to a ridge: a thick understory, boles upright and leaning, crowded with ferns and woven with climbers; and above, the crowns of tall trees.

Nitti looks at him and laughs—a carefree laugh, the laugh of a child. But there was something practiced about it. She asks about his adventures in other countries, flattering and teasing, as if he's led a life of indulging his whims. He plays along, saying that he works as little as possible, always has time to play the lothario, and receives the attentions of a Casanova wherever he lands.

"I'm younger than you are," Nitti points out.

"I'll be a good guide," he replies.

"You're just trying to say the right words."

"Were those the right ones?" he asks.

A half-smile, curious, knowing. "Women are fools for men like you."

They study each other.

"You have dangerous eyes," Nitti says.

"Why dangerous?"

"Do you want something alcoholic?"

Kell wonders if there is liquor in Nitti's home.

"I will if you will," he says.

"I don't drink."

"You're Muslim."

"It's not that," she says.

"You want to be in control," he guesses. He sets his hand on the veranda rail.

"I do," she replies, putting her hand over his, as if to make her control explicit.

Across the river, a rustling reaches them. Kell spots the whipping branches. A troop of monkeys—dusky langurs with white eye rings—are leaping through the tree crowns. Beside the river, a stork-billed kingfisher, apricot and blue, rises from a sapling with a scarlet screech. Nitti's hand is caressing his.

For real affection, he thinks, the magnetism had to be equal—a woman had to be as attracted to him as he was to her. The wariness from their first meeting is gone. Nitti seems relaxed, in good spirits, but— How authentic is this advance? With how many men had agreements been struck?

"What are you thinking?" she asks.

"I'm wondering," Kell says, "who was here on this veranda before me."

"This was your choice," she reminds him.

"I'm just curious."

"His name was Amin," she says. "He was smart and good-looking but short. It wasn't love, but we were friends. Good friends, if that's what you're asking."

"How long were you together?" Kell says.

"Almost a year."

He nods slowly, trying to imagine. "Thanks. For being honest."

Below them, the river zags between boulders, dishing over a pale slab. He can see the fenced borders of an untended orchard with bananas, papayas and rambutans.

Where the river looped, the house jutted out. A window is lit.

"The waterside wing," Nitti says.

To the left, farther downstream, the current slides through a sluice, hissing and swirling beneath arching palms and twisted lianas.

"Soothing," he mutters.

"There's a swamp that way."

Nitti takes her hand from his. When he looks up, her lips are humorless, her eyes deep. Thunder sounds in the distance, and in response, the langurs gabble to each other. They know what thunder means.

Kell moves closer, invading the space between them. Nitti draws a quick breath. Her lids close, and his lips touch hers.

A world opens for him—the world of another—as broad and as thick as any jungle on earth; and, for being the threshold of a human heart, so much more welcoming. *Nitti*, he thinks, and *Nitti* again.

This will be no "arrangement." Kell feels certain of that.

He's in the green mesh enclosure, standing beside one of his lab assistants, examining a print-out of sequence profiles for edited torch gingers well into the growing phase.

"How's F-238?" Kell asks.

The assistant turns and points at a leafless stem, three feet tall with a swollen bud at its top. "Blissful," she says, approaching it. She touches the bud, angling it toward him. "Like a slitted pupil, don't you think?"

Kell laughs. To the ginger explant, they had knocked in

genes from the eye of a local tree frog.

On the path below, a dozen monkeys have corralled a group of tourists. Some of the animals are begging, holding their hands out. One jumps onto a man's shoulder and shrieks. When the man drops his sandwich, the monkeys gather around it to fight for the spoils. Kell checks the hour. He'd risen that morning with Nitti in his thoughts, and she's been there all day. Now finally, it's time to leave. He removes his lab coat, bids his staff goodbye, and heads for the Gardens' parking lot.

He reaches Ipoh and the house by the river at sundown. As Kell pulls onto the apron, he sees an older Chinese man working a pair of tarnished shears, pruning the small trees around the house while he hums to himself. As Kell approaches, the gardener smiles. He has no front teeth.

This time it is Susilo who spies him through the louvers. He directs Kell to the right stair.

At the top, the old man welcomes him. "Are you hungry?" he asks.

The elderly woman stands in her smock two feet away, silent, dour as before, smelling like furniture oil and antiseptics. "Prawan can fix you something," Susilo offers.

When Kell declines, the housekeeper steps away. Nitti is seated by the low table, speaking to a man in a jade suit. Her hair is hanging free in thick black waves. She and the man rise together as Susilo canes toward them.

"Our new friend," Susilo says, introducing Kell.

The man in the jade suit extends his hand in the Western way.

Nitti introduces the man, Kell hears the word "doctor," and he shakes the man's hand. The doctor's polite enough, but his smile is forced. Considering me, Kell thinks. Guessing, judging— Then the doctor is saying goodbye, and Susilo is leading him toward the right stair.

On the table is a document. Kell watches Nitti stoop and retrieve it. She puts her arm through his and escorts him out of the guest room, down a corridor. At the corridor's end, the walls open around them, hung with tapestries. She turns to a door on her right, opens it and invites him inside.

An armoire, a gold-trimmed vanity with an oval mirror, a bed large enough for two, and a window with bamboo blinds. Her room.

Nitti sets the document on the vanity and pulls a fresh hibiscus from a vase. She looks over her shoulder at him. "What if I refused you now?" she says.

Her expression is tentative, as if she is asking herself the question. Kell doesn't respond. She's toying with him, he thinks. But the toying hurts. In the vanity mirror, he sees her raise the document and slide the hibiscus stem under the clip. Then she turns and hands papers and blossom to him.

"What's this?" He lifts the scarlet petals to see.

It's a medical report in English. A gynecology exam with an STD panel.

"Are you pleased?" Nitti asks.

Kell meets her gaze, hearing and seeing her cynical edge. She's been demeaned, he thinks, and he's part of it. Kell sighs, feeling the magnetism wither to nothing.

26

Silence. Nitti watches him. He looks away.

"Let's go out," she suggests.

Disengaged, glum and apathetic now, he obliges her.

They go in his car. The place she chooses is a ten-minute drive. She says little; and he, not a word. Fortunately the traffic is light, because Kell's attention isn't on the wheel. He's feeling the transaction acutely, considering the many questions his "gift" posed. His dismay fills the air between them like a bad cologne.

Nitti directs him where to park. They leave the car, walking beneath covered arcades, not touching, not speaking. Kell had been to Ipoh's Old Town before. The city was trying to revive it. Cafes and galleries had sprouted among the markets and kopitiams. Storefronts and alleyways, weathered and chipped, had been thinly overpainted. The treatment was meant to look stylish, but the decay showed through.

Nitti ushers him down a narrow lane into an eatery. The hostess struggles with her English, and when they're seated, the waitress is worse. Kell can't understand what she's saying, so Nitti makes the selections. A few minutes later, the food arrives. Kell is polite, reserved.

While they eat, silence divides them. Midway through the meal, he sighs and proposes they go their separate ways.

"I'm sorry," he says.

Nitti shakes her head.

He looks past her. "I shouldn't have imagined—"

"It was the doctor's report," she says.

Kell doesn't answer.

"Are you angry with me?" she asks.

"No. It was my mistake—"

"Stay with me tonight," she says. "I promise—"

"Nitti—"

"Don't do this." She's pleading now.

"Nitti," he sighs. "It's really love— That's what I'm looking for."

"I know," a spasm of sobs wells up. "I know," she says. "I know, I know."

Her eyes are brimming. "We can't give the money back."

"I'm not asking you to. The fault is mine—"

In the car, headed back, Nitti seems beaten; then, as they approach the house by the river, grimly determined. She keeps her silence, eyes red, hands in her lap.

When he parks on the leaf-littered apron, she remains in her seat while he turns the ignition off. Kell exits the car, circles and opens the passenger door. Nitti grabs his wrist as she rises. Crossing the apron, she wraps her arm around his, like a liana with bloody sap, clinging tightly.

They take the back stair and climb to a dark landing. An inside light is on.

Nitti opens the door, grasps his hand and starts down the corridor. Kell's steps are grudging. He's going to resist, to excuse himself.

They reach her bedroom, and he plants himself at the threshold.

"I'm not going in," he says.

"Don't be afraid," she says.

Kell doesn't reply.

"Hold on to me," Nitti says.

Kell moves his free hand to loosen her clasp.

"No," she protests, and he can feel her strength; at the same time, a weaker sound churns in her chest. She's after control, but she's struggling as well to soften herself. "Can't you understand?" Her voice is muted, like the purr of a leopard cat. "I want love too."

That's not love I'm hearing, Kell thinks.

"Don't leave," she says. Nitti's dark eyes are big before him. She's using the pause, turning the knob.

Unbalanced, urged forward, he crosses the threshold.

By Nitti's vanity, a candle is burning. There's a bowl of sectioned starfruit on the bedstand. Without a word, she begins to disrobe.

Kell raises his hands, palms toward her.

She's unbuttoning her blouse. Bronze light flickers across her shoulders. She drapes the blouse over her vanity stool, ribs shifting like sago spines.

What are you doing? he asks himself.

She reaches behind to unfasten her bra.

Her vertebral groove is shadowed, then the knobs appear as she shifts.

The bra comes free, and Nitti turns.

"How am I?" she asks, her voice tremulous as a child's.

Her nipples are stippled like gecko skin, rugose around the tips.

Leave, Kell thinks. Turn and leave.

"I'm alone," she says. Unaffected, naïve. Fearful but needy. She slides off her skirt.

A shiver between his shoulders invades the back of his head.

Nitti raises her hands and begins to unbutton his shirt.

Kell tries to push her away, but the push is weak.

She fingers the waistband of her panties, and the fabric rolls down her thighs.

She's as hairless as a child.

"For you," she whispers, stepping closer.

Her smooth mons is like the flesh of a doll.

She knows how to arouse men, and that's what she's doing. She's unfastening his belt. He does nothing to stop her.

You're a fool, he berates himself. The fact that he'd paid, and the absence of real emotion, would pain him when it was over.

Nitti prods his hip, guiding him toward the bed.

She crawls onto the mattress. He follows, and they stretch out together.

Nitti's fingers cross his chest. Kell puts his hand on her waist, doing his best to act familiar, though there is nothing whatever to feel familiar about.

She touches his middle. He strokes her back.

Then her fingers spider toward his groin.

The instinct of lust emerges from hibernation, opening its eyes and looking around. Nitti's face is in darkness now, the candle behind her. She's focused, regardful perhaps. Or crafty, absent expression. Or perhaps she has no face at all—the wavy hair is only a shell. If the woman in his arms has no awareness—no thoughts or feelings—what does it matter?

A whining reaches him—faint, high-pitched, at the limit of hearing. The niggling of conscience. A signal to leave.

It's the fruit on the bedstand. A nimbus of gnats is hovering over it. In the flickering candlelight, he can see them like jungle spores come alive, drifting around Nitti's hollow head. A dance of dots, a weaving of threads. A veil with no face to cover. Or a diaphanous fabric, meant to be shaped.

I'm a tailorbird, Kell thinks, sewing leaves with strands of silk. An army of weaver ants knitting a nest. A botanist splicing genes, trying to fashion the lover he wants. Making the best of a bad situation.

He can no longer hear Nitti's breath. There is only the whining of gnats, the thrum of threads, the hum of a river. Wriggling leeches and empty webs. Beads of rain on a moonlit window, frog spawn floating on a moonlit pool.

The woman beside him rocks onto her back, knees bent, thighs reflexed, flesh smooth and rubbery.

A frog in the jungle.

Can a man find bliss with a frog? He can if he's not too proud. A frog on a trembling leaf, spotted and streaked; a frog in the mud, eyes bulbed, lips on your cheek; a frog in a tree, stuck on a branch, eyes slitted and sultry, or leaping into the air, harlequin-pink.

This frog has her calves by his neck, knees bent on either side of his head, legs folded over his shoulders. Has he teased the amphibian from her? Through the dark and damp and caught breath, he feels her advance.

Or he imagines it. They are animals, creatures, strangers.

31

But— Impelled by lust, by instinct, the freedom of blindness, he's straining toward her. Is she with him, doing the same, taking the risk?

Doubt, trepidation— The fear of knowing too much. Close, very close. He senses it, even as his belly and loins are warmed by the froggy basket. His hands slide down the froggy thighs, through the mucid flume and around her backside where it's soft and fleshy.

Froggy hands hold his head, knobby digits tangle his hair. Sighing or hissing, ape or amphibian, what does it matter? His chest expands, gulping the air, lunging, gasping. The frog's middle is silky, her heart nippled, her insides slick— He's in the water with her, stroking in tandem, frogging across the moonlit pool—

Who are you? at the back of his mind.

But closer, closer; together, so very close now—

Then a reflex shock, muscles lock and spasm. And, with a suck and croak, the wogging issue pours out of him, blanching the water.

Breathless, sweating, a marshy wallow, a ceiling of clouds.

Kell's arm folds. He rolls onto his hip, shedding his distortions.

Frogs, he thinks. Cute, clammy, delicate, alien—

Was it something in her, sordid, alluring? Had he launched a parody to lighten his self-condemnation? Or was it only the eye of F-238, slitted at the back of his mind?

A sliver of moon appears in the window. She's on the bed, inches away, silent, half on her side with her knees still bent. Kell slides his arm beneath her neck and grasps her thigh, rotating her toward him. Frogs, reflexed and croaking. He can see her face now, bowed nose, mussed hair, the moonlit eyes impossibly deep.

Contact. There is contact, strange as it is.

Kell edges closer. He kisses her lips, and something seems to relax inside her.

And now, as the kiss draws out, her legs lengthen, her thighs touch his.

He places his palm on Nitti's middle, feeling the soft flesh of her belly. He kisses her again, and Nitti—a beautiful creature no caring soul would deny—whispers to him, caressing his temple.

"*Sayang*," she says.

He doesn't know the word, but her fragility pierces his heart.

"*Terima, terima.*"

How could he have considered leaving? She wants the same thing he does. He kisses her nape, her ear, her neck. He moves his hand under her waist, circles her trunk and holds her close, settling his head with his lips to her ear. With this woman, he sighs, love is entering his life.

Nitti stiffens. It's as if his sigh stopped her.

She's murmuring now, a sound of reserve.

"*Jangan*," she says. Regret, discomfort.

She wants to be open, but there is something held back.

Amid the promise and the nascent hope is Kell's perception of some kind of blockage. In this, their first moment of real contact, Nitti is a bloom not yet free of its bud, a hatchling still in its egg, an insect not yet emerged from its molt.

2

The next morning Kell wakes in Nitti's bed. She is stretched beside him, facing the window. Through it he sees a bounty of green hills, tangled slopes and marshy valleys.

He touches her nape, puts his hand on her shoulder.

They rise together and, without speaking, they dress.

In the dining room, Prawan serves them coconut rice. Their quiet persists until the housekeeper leaves. Then Nitti sets her spoon down.

"Last night—" Her eyes search his.

Kell waits.

"The way you held me—" She's barely audible.

"I was in a strange state," he says. "I imagined you were . . . a jungle creature."

She blinks, nervous, uncertain.

"A cute one," he says. "A tree frog."

Her lids flare and she laughs.

"I felt close to you."

"And I to you," she says.

"You found the innocence in me: the boy who marvels at wild things."

"You were very emotional," Nitti says.

The dark eyes watch him.

"We need love," Kell says, "but only the child inside us can receive it."

She considers his words.

"It comes back to that, doesn't it? When we're young," he says, "we're open. And we expect the best with good reason— most animals have caring mothers."

Nitti looks at her rice, mulling his words or bothered by them.

"There's plenty of science on the subject," he says.

"Did you have one?"

"One what?"

"A caring mother."

"I did," Kell says. "Tender. Mindful. Devoted. She wasn't tough enough. When my father left us, she retreated from life. She was ruled by fear, and the closer I came to manhood, the more threatened she felt. But when I was young, I was loved. Her heart was open to me and I trusted her."

He speaks the next words slowly. "It wasn't that way with my wife."

"Tell me," she says.

"We were grownups together," Kell says, "but we couldn't

be kids. Commitment we had. But no play, no spirit, no depth. There was no younger version of us."

Nitti is silent.

After a minute, she sighs to herself. Then softly:

"With men, you might say I've been guarded. Distant. Not trusting. I know what trust is. I knew love too, when I was a child. Protected. Cared for."

"Did you feel that way with me last night?"

She's silent, her face unexpressive. Remembering her feelings perhaps, or reluctant to share them.

North of Ipoh, at a fishing village named Nibong Tebal, a small river flows into the sea. Kell knew a man there, a marine biologist who owned a small boat, and when Kell asked for a favor, the man agreed.

Two days after their first night together, Kell drove Nitti to Taiping for dinner; and when they finished, he surprised her. They continued north to Nibong and met the man at the dock.

The boat is moored at the river's edge. The man climbs into the stern and fires the engine while Kell and Nitti seat themselves on a thwart by the bow. As the boat creeps away from the dock, nightjars call from the shoreline scrub, lift into the air and fly inland.

Kell circles her waist with his arm. She responds in kind, hugging his shoulder, putting her hand on his leg. They watch the long ripples on the water's surface wrap around the boat as it turns. Spicules of mist frost their cheeks, and the engine hum joins the *whishing* as they head downstream. With the pilot in the stern, lost in shadow, the craft seems to move magically, driven by desire or impulse alone.

The lights from dwellings disappear behind them. The silhouettes of trees on the banks rise through the night on either side; and then, as the boat reaches the river's mouth, within those dark silhouettes, dots of light begin to wink and sparkle. Kell extends his arm, pointing.

"I see them," she whispers.

Pteroptyx beetles throng the berembang trees. Drunk with yearning, flashing with hope or hunger or whatever they felt.

A fish owl hoots. The boat's hull scrapes the branches, then the motor dies and the bow nudges the bank. The golden blinking surrounds them now.

Kell puts his lips to Nitti's. Her hand presses his pectoral, matching his feeling. They breathe as one, touching their tongues, sharing their natures, joining the signaling of spirits in the branching bush.

It is more, much more than Kell expects. An open portal. A headlong plunge, a covenant of trembling, fragile but fearless. As the kiss draws out, it grows in intensity, pointed and ample, infused with the movements of the blinking creatures. The jots squirm toward each other, linger and drift apart, as if driven by the surge and subsiding of deep emotion. And then, as if all the world is caught up in the moment, thunder sounds and the sky blinks too, a storm brewing over the sea beyond the mouth of the river.

Cracks, deep booms. The pilot speaks and the boat shakes. He's fired the engine, he's turning the bow away from the bank.

A minute later, they're headed back, speeding upriver. As quickly as it started, the storm fades. There is only the motor's hum and the blinking of stars in the sky. One of them is falling, Kell sees: a plane is landing, returning to earth. His arm is around Nitti, holding her close.

The next afternoon, Kell is in the Ginger House lab, creating a plasmid from an actias moon moth he'd netted the week before. He'd snipped off the hind wing tips and put them in a small tube with a pair of glass beads. After freezing the tube, he'd used a shaker to pulverize the moth tissue and a centrifuge to spin out its DNA. A lab tech had run PCR tests to amplify the genes Kell wants to use, and he's pipetting the amplified gene now, adding Cas9 and *Agrobacterium* for transfection in an electroporator. In less than a second, the shock will insert the moth genes into the explant of a spiral ginger.

Kell's phone chimes. He sets the tube down, removes a glove and slides the mobile from his pocket.

It's Nitti. A tender greeting, then she invites him to stay with her the following weekend. "There's something I want to show you," she says.

On Saturday morning, Kell crosses the bridge from Penang to the mainland. He enters Ipoh beneath a clear sky, sunlight flashing on the limestone knobs and vaulted hills. When he pulls onto the apron, Nitti is at a window waving him toward the octagon.

The door opens and she embraces him with a breezy smile. She's wearing a white blouse, linen pants and jungle boots. He'd dressed for a hike at her request.

"Ready?" she says.

She leads him back down the stair, around the house to a shed. Twists of periwinkle are rooted in the cracked stucco, and the little pink flowers are blooming.

Nitti steps inside. "We'll take a parang."

She selects a big-bladed machete with a silvered edge and hands it to him. "You know how to use it," she guesses. Kell nods.

He follows her through the untended orchard to the path that verges the river. As the flow comes into view—the glassy skirts, the tumbles and froth—Kell hears a scream. He lifts his head, and they watch a rusty kite dive through the blue into the jungle on the river's far side.

"Hurry along," Nitti says.

She has some purpose, something important she wants to share.

A stick insect with pink wings flies between them, settles on a shrub and turns into a twig. As they round a bend, the ringing of cicadas mounts. A small troop of macaques is gathered in a stand of flowering cloves. Two are grooming each other. A large male approaches Kell, testy, sauntering. Nitti points at a nursing infant. The mother holds the newborn with a furry arm while it sucks on her dug.

A minute later, they reach a slat bridge.

"We cross here," she says, stepping onto the swaying span, boots clacking.

On the far side, beyond a grove of wild banana, the jungle's green barricade rises. As they enter the dense growth, scores of voices greet them, whistling, clicking, rasping and buzzing. Rain had been heavy the night before, and the boughs are still dripping. Kell swings the parang, clearing vines and saplings.

"Where are we going?"

"A special place," she replies.

A butterfly sails between them, its orange wings framed in black, margins scribbled and toothed.

"A cethosia," Kell says.

"A freed soul," Nitti smiles.

The trees are taller and the crowns thicker. The jungle grows shaded and cooler, a profusion of smells wafting around them: sodden moss, acrid lichen, a burst of floral perfume, mold and defecation. There's no path here, but Nitti moves without hesitation, finding a way through spiny rattans, stilted roots and thorny lianas as thick as their legs. The weave is tight. You couldn't spot an anglehead lizard or a langur whole; you'd peer through chinks for an eye or a tail.

"Do you see them?" she says.

Kell parts two giant tear-shaped leaves and steps through. A stand of trees rises before them, trunks vividly hued, tan and apricot, ocher and rust, all barked with the same elongated puzzle pattern.

"They haven't changed," she says. "Every tree is exactly as it was when I was little. The same color, the same pattern, the same size. Put your hand on one."

Kell does as she asks, feeling how cool and smooth it is. "They're tropical eucalyptus," he says. "They're growing, but very slowly."

The trees are hard as iron, leaves long and fledged like arrows where they attach to the stems. Kell points. On an amber bough, a scarlet trogon looks down like a sentinel, watching them both.

"It's a library," Nitti says. "Can you see?"

He can't. And then he can: there are documents everywhere. The ground is covered with bark curls, and around the trunks scrolls are tented and piled, like ancient texts read and discarded.

They continue forward, boots rustling the scrolls, crossing the sanctum of vanished sages till they reach the edge of the grove.

"It's just ahead," Nitti says.

She speaks in a muted voice, like a child sharing a secret; and Kell responds, feeling a welling regard and camaraderie.

The undergrowth is dense here, so he takes the lead, swinging the parang. Vines are woven tightly, twisted and braiding; the boles are slick and the fronds are glossed. Without warning, the wind picks up, carrying droplets that freckle their faces.

"Kell—"

There's excitement in her voice. When he looks, Nitti's cheeks are glistening and a wet lock hangs by her ear.

"See it?" she says.

A tan hump of hill appears, its front wafered, its crown bushy-headed. Lower down, beyond a covert of wild cinnamon, a mouth gapes—a black hollow with pale lips. The Kinta limestone is riddled with caves.

Nitti moves in front of him now, leading the way between crossed boughs and dangling leaves, pink and green. She halts before the opening.

"Clap," she says, "three times."

With each nod of her head, they clap their hands.

"To scare off the evil spirits," she says.

On a lip of rock above the cave's mouth, swiftlets roost, tittering and clicking, coming and going. The two of them clamber over the broken threshold, the day behind, their dim silhouettes looming on the pale walls, bigger than life. With every step, the arch seems lower, the mouth seems to close; the angle of light changes, and they are shrinking together, smaller and smaller, until their shadowy selves are like shuffling dwarves.

Nitti pauses and draws a candle from her pocket, and when the candle is lit, she leads the way into the dark interior. Stalactite bosses gleam on a wall, pointed and dripping; fringes and pipes, folded drapes, rippling veils. There are holes in the ceiling above—circular holes, the bottoms of wells. "Here," she murmurs, heading up a slump and around a blind corner. She raises the flame, lighting a wall with glittering gills. Below them, stalactites lie in pieces, fallen from a beam like teeth from a jaw.

"I was seven," Nitti says. "There was a boy. We would come here together."

Kell hears her hesitation and the echo of a wistful memory.

"Taseen was his name," she says. "He called it 'the Temple' because it's like Sam Poh's cave."

"I've been there," Kell says. Sam Poh was a monk.

"No one knew about this one but us." Nitti motions him forward.

"Look." She raises the candle. On the wall before him, Kell sees a fossil scallop with rays spread like the fingers of a reaching hand.

She waves the light, continuing forward. "He was always making things up." They're in a room, Kell sees, and the room has pockets—alcoves where children might huddle and whisper.

Past a boss built by a hundred slops, alongside an eave with hanging needles. It's perfectly humid now and their skin is slicked. She halts before a four-foot stalagmite. Kell comes up beside her.

Nitti turns and kisses his cheek, regarding him silently. Then she sets her free hand on the stalagmite's nose.

"We cleanse ourselves," she says.

She raises her palm, wet with the dripstone's water, and washes her face. He follows her example.

Beyond the dripstone, Nitti turns down a gleaming corridor and enters a larger cavern with ribbed walls and a high fluked ceiling. At its center, a helical pillar stands. The pillar's turnings are studded with stalactite clusters, all finned and dripping. It's like something pulled from a giant's gut.

At the base of the pillar, a niche appears.

"The Secret Chamber," Nitti says.

She stoops and crawls in. Kell follows, squirming onto a shelf beside her.

Nitti sets the candle on a scorched bracket.

The niche is narrow and tent-like, walls hung with gills and streaked with damp. The shadows cast by the wavering flame make the space collapse and expand.

"It's smaller than it used to be," Nitti murmurs.

He can hear her breathing. And he can feel her relief—her calm, her peace. It's as if they have entered a hidden dimension, an interior place where the threats of the world would never reach you.

"Do you know the expression '*budi bahasa*'?" she asks.

Kell shakes his head.

"It's the sensing of things beneath the surface. Subtle things. That's what I felt the night at the Qing Club. 'Budi bahasa.' The power of things unspoken."

Her words puzzle him. "You were frightened."

"I was," she sighs.

"What frightened you?"

Nitti takes a breath. "You reminded me of Taseen."

Kell frowns. Then he recalls the moment and replays it for her—the élan from his youth: a wave of his hand, a naïve smile with wondering eyes.

Nitti looks as if she'd been struck. Her shoulders sag, her lips tremble.

Kell reaches for her hand and clasps it.

"Taseen—" She's trying to explain, but she speaks his name with a groan. Then she seems to lapse into her past. "I miss you," she says, "I miss you." A small white moth is fluttering beside Nitti's brow. "I'm so sad," she says, speaking now to Kell and herself.

"We played 'Strangers,'" she tries to smile. "No one could tell who we were. They didn't recognize us."

Kell holds her hand tightly, his eyes on hers.

"We didn't change inside," she explains, "we just looked different, and only we knew. Once we disappeared," she says. "We were invisible. No one could see us. With Taseen, I was—"

She looks away.

"You were what?" he asks.

Her chest is heaving. "Losing him—"

Kell sees a tear descending her cheek.

"I want love too," Nitti says.

He still has hold of her hand.

A long moment passes. Then she speaks again.

"Will you ever find the one you're looking for?"

Silence in the Secret Chamber.

"I think I've found her," Kell says.

She turns half toward him.

"I could be your Temple, Nitti."

Her dark eyes seem suddenly plumbless, and her smile is

like a child's. It seems that a powerful love—true and private—has been set loose around them.

He lifts his fingers to blot her tears, and a shadow arm climbs the wall, circling the chamber. She sees it and flinches, huddling aside.

Kell watches her, hand still raised, frozen midair. The movement frightened her, and it was more than a reflex. She felt threatened—even here, in this hidden place.

He wants to reassure her, to calm her fears. But she's turned, and she's clambering out of the Chamber.

They cross the large cavern slowly, in silence.

A few minutes later, they are out in the open again, squinting at the jungle around them.

As they start back, a mournful sound comes from the sky. A white-bellied eagle is circling down. The bird spreads its wings and lands on the rim of a nest in the crotch of a pulai tree. Then it calls again.

"Crying for her mate," Nitti says.

The pulai trunk is buttressed and deeply fluted, and the nest is made of thick branches. Kell wonders if it was there when Nitti was young.

"What happened to Taseen?" he asks.

"He didn't have a choice," she says. "His father got a job in Kelantan."

Her voice trails off.

As they approach the river, it begins to rain. Kell uses the parang to cut free a heart-shaped elephant ear, and he holds it over them both.

They spent the rest of that day in bed together. For Kell, intimacy with Nitti was like holding on to something precious and then losing your grip, expecting it to land with a crash; and then finding that somehow the object hadn't fallen; it was suspended, intact, eager for the shelter of his arms if he would only reach out.

Rapture, confusion. Alone, at risk, almost forgotten; then abruptly restored, remembered, and with a kiss from the heart, taken back. He began to understand: there was a difference between Nitti-the-woman and Nitti-the-child. They could both be buoyant or frightened; both might embrace or recoil from him, but in different ways.

Nitti-the-woman could be cunning—pleading, servile—or she could be bold; if the impulse gripped her, she wasn't afraid to make demands. Then her unease would surface; he'd see an eclipse in her face and the germination of thoughts—thoughts she'd keep hidden, and words you would never hear.

Nitti-the-child was simpler. She wanted badly to be honest and open with him, and she shared kind thoughts, immature jests, feelings wringing and deep. But there were troubling thoughts too. Nitti-the-child needed love as much as the child in him. But there were dangers for her that Kell didn't understand; dangers that he might unwittingly expose her to. With these fearful things, Nitti imagined she was on her own. Amid his concerns about her, Kell thought of himself. Her vacillations were painful. The more he cared about her, the more risk he felt.

A breeze makes the gauzy drapes billow. The fabric is tinged with twilight gold. Night is falling. Naked, Nitti crosses the floor, returning to the bed.

Kell opens his arms, and her body folds against him.

A kiss, a soft kiss. Her hand is a bird that lands on his chest, stroking his pectoral with her wing. Kell scuttles his fingers behind her, making a treeshrew that—very gently—climbs her spine. Nitti shrugs while his kisses land. Then the shrew reaches the base of her neck and she falls to giggling, while the bird hops over his belly.

He slides one arm behind her shoulder and the other between her legs, cradling her, lifting her. "Kell," she sighs. Her rear is silky, its divide like the midrib of a leaf, cheeks yielding as his hand rides between them. Her shoulders, her thighs, her rippling sides, smooth, so very smooth—river rock polished by seasonless water, water that had never stopped flowing through the oldest jungle in the world.

She's reveling in his caresses, loosing whimpers and gasps that slice and scissor and turn in midair, as fast as feeding swallows. Nitti spreads her arms now, not to receive him, but to yield herself up.

"You're my boy," she says.

"You're my girl," he replies.

Without a knock, the door opens.

Prawan steps forward holding a silver tray, undaunted by their entanglement.

Kell reaches for the bedsheet and pulls it to his waist.

Nitti doesn't react—there's no sign of shock or agitation.

The housekeeper takes a glass of water from the tray and passes it to Nitti. Then she edges toward the vanity, sets her tray down and opens the vanity drawer. She retrieves a drugstore jar and removes a pill.

Nitti holds her palm out and receives it with her head bowed. As Kell watches, she puts the pill on her tongue and drinks from the glass to swallow it down.

Prawan checks the pitcher. "Shall I—"

"No, we're fine." Nitti sets the empty glass on the bedstand.

With that, the housekeeper turns and exits the room. Kell listens to the soles of her sandals clapping against her heels, wondering at what he's witnessed.

"She's very free with you," he says. "And us."

Nitti's quiet as a mouse deer.

"Can I ask what you're taking?" Kell says.

All at once she's a creature being hunted, crouched among twigs and branches. She turns to face the open window.

The river's susurrus reaches them, the rasps of crickets, the burping of toads. Kell puts his hand on her wrist and feels it stiffen. The child, the carefree girl, is frightened. And now—for whatever reason—she's being shuttered away.

Nitti-the-woman raises herself and closes the window.

"Wasps," she says.

There are two on her pillow and a half-dozen more in the air between them. Night wasps are swarming some-where nearby.

Kell leaves the bed, grabs his shoes and, with one in each hand, begins crushing the hovering insects. Nitti retrieves her slippers and does the same.

As the last orange body falls to the floor, she faces him.

"Like you," she says.

Kell ticks his head, not understanding.

"Looking for a new home," Nitti says.

He brushes a dead wasp from the sole of his shoe. "I hope I have better luck."

She returns to the mattress, kneeing across it, reaching for him. She manacles his wrists with her hands, pulling him toward her, jaw set, dragging him across the bed, then forcing him onto his back and hovering over him straight-armed, breasts pointed down.

Nitti kisses him, but her lips are sealed, and he can feel her teeth behind them. Her innocence is like the tail a gecko has shed. This is the Nitti who'd faced him across the table in the Qing Club—aloof, suspicious, with a reflexive antipathy.

She's straddling him now, knees on either side. She's not inviting him in, but she isn't barring the way either. Kell grasps her hips and forces her down.

It's a new lust for them—grave, dark and narrow, absent endearments. Nitti gives him a whiff of scorn, then grudging acceptance— Instead of cooling his ardor, her reluctance piques it. He's crossed the threshold, entered her body. But despite the fact that he feels her heat, he realizes: there's a deeper threshold. The door to her heart is elsewhere, unopened, and there's a child behind it, listening.

Nitti looms over him, arms and legs planted like the aerial roots of a strangler fig. The roots, he imagines, are grafting together, building a prison around him; and that magnifies his desire. He's a captive—adoring, enraged at being so unable, enlarging himself inside her restraints, boiling to rise.

He knows jungle rules from his science, and she knows them from life—although the history of her learning is still opaque to him. Kell grapples her shoulders, pulling her down. He claws her waist, thumbs digging in, a spiny rattan daggering up an unwilling trunk. He closes his jaw on her bicep, gnawing a bough; rolls her onto her hip, and like a parasite climber overtopping its host, he pulls himself over her, shading her out.

Through the leafy darkness, he sees Nitti's eyes: two points of light approaching. She's strange to him now, a wild creature flouting the earth—a winged lizard, a flying snake, a caped colugo— And he's the bug-eyed tarsier on a naked bole, trembling, clinging—

"Nitti," he whispers, feeling deceived, yearning for the purer spirit.

For an instant, he sees it: a perfect creature, glowing gold but no longer human. She's a cicada molt stuck to a tree, like her successor in every detail, but empty, hollow, devoid of life.

Nitti's freed herself, she's rising again, clambering over him, humped like a tortoise, reaching her hands, his hair in her fists. The creature he's struggling with is hardened, incensed with a spiteful desire and grimly demanding.

If she's speaking, Kell barely hears. His ears are thronged by simian grunts, stuttering insects and shrieking birds. Her trunk is erect, towering over him. High above, he sees the two points of light, fixed and severe.

He can feel her thighs on either side of his head, and he knows what she wants. Distant love, abasing love, ministrations without fond words or foolish regard. She wants him to honor her harshness, and if he has needs of his own, he can manage that himself.

Kell bows to her demands.

From the jungle come the hoots of a night heron, the moan of a clouded leopard, the chucks of a terrified monkey. And the two points of light—

Nitti is a giant tarantula, descending from a billowing tube of web, her eyes glowing. He's crossed the line, and her trip wire is trembling.

She shakes, her arms dart around him, imagining she'll send her sharp fangs into him and suck his essence.

But Kell isn't going to be prey.

He's shifted, he's hardened. He's using his length to slide out of harm's way. Not a bug in a tree, food for a spider, but a cryptic snake, invisible, hidden in darkness, watching the drama from the forest floor.

Is it rain or distant music? Music playing, perhaps, at the back of his mind. A pattering, rhythmic, resonant and—listening carefully—tuneful. A gentle descent of arms and mallets, a bedtime jingle played on a toy marimba. Through the modest drops sound random scratchings, whirrings, chirps. Then gradually, subtly, the downpour mounts. The bug sounds fade. The mallets beat firmly, the patter turns into a pounding.

There's a storm outside, beyond the window. Boughs in the orchard whip, and the river below sighs and wheezes.

Half asleep, Kell feels for Nitti, touches her blindly. Then he opens his eyes.

She's on her side, a nostril budging with silent breath, her hand curled like a girl's beside her cheek. Kell lifts his shoulder, rising slowly over her. He lowers his lips and kisses her brow. Beneath the lid, her eye is shifting. Lost in dream.

Was she back in the Temple, hiding in the Secret Chamber with Taseen or himself? The rain comes still harder, flooding the roof, hugging the room. In the jungle, he thinks, the trunks are shuddering and the lianas are banging.

Then, as Kell lowers himself and leans back on his side, Nitti gasps. Her middle twists as if something has hold of it and is squeezing. Her arms squirm, her knees flex. Beneath her lids, the dreaming eyes twitch.

As he watches, Nitti's lips part, and a scraping noise comes from her throat. She seems to be struggling for breath. A choking groan, her trunk buckles, and when she tries to draw air again, she's unable.

Kell puts his hands on her shoulders, ready to wake her. The room is shivering, the rain's a deluge. In the jungle, the humus is drenched and the swamps flooding; the tree crowns are crabs, their arms reaching out.

Nitti's near leg jerks, while the other pedals, as if trying to get away from something. Her body is arching and crimping from some malfunction that can't be interrupted and must be endured.

Kell shakes her. "Nitti—"

But she doesn't wake. Her head bucks, neck craning, mouth gaping wide. She's choking, panicked, gagged by a terror she can't expel.

Kell shakes her again. Nitti's lids part, and a full-throated scream fills the room.

"Wake up." He cradles her shoulders and raises her.

Nitti's eyes are fixed and staring. Can she see him through the darkness? She twists, recoiling, knees hitched, jaw spasming. Is she awake?

She screams again—at him, as if he's the one who's threatening her, as if he has followed her out of her dream.

"Please—" He shakes her fiercely now. She's kicking and flailing her arms, thrashing her hair, refusing. What does she imagine he wants?

"You're safe," he says, "you can breathe, you're awake—"

Has she heard him? Her gape remains, but the scream is gone, and spasms in her trunk are subsiding. She's no longer breathless, no longer fighting.

She can hear him, he thinks. She knows he's trying to calm her, assure her, comfort her. She slumps onto her side, limp, yielding.

Nitti's eyes frighten him. They're open, staring, but not at him. She's aware he's there, isn't she? An imploring sound rises, faintly, in her throat.

Then her eyes close.

After that, there is silence. Silence and stillness.

The rain is no longer pounding. The storm has ended, and so has the struggle beside him.

Nitti lies motionless in the darkness, looking stiff and cold.

Light divides the curtains.

Kell opens his eyes, seeing Nitti curled beside him, still asleep, her dark hair draped over her shoulder. Her lips are parted, and the tail of her mouth is kinked as if she's remembering something. An innocent, untroubled face. The fears that beset her the previous night are gone.

He eases his legs over the mattress edge, puts his feet on the floor and is about to stand when he catches sight of an object on the bedstand: a child's toy, a white goose with orange feet. He picks it up and the rubber body compresses between his fingers, releasing a honk.

He looks at Nitti, sees the noise hasn't wakened her, then he puts the toy back on the bedstand and rises. Naked, he makes his way into the bathroom.

The air is warm, the tiles cool to his feet. He turns on the shower, and when the temp is stable, he steps in.

The spray prickles his chest. He soaps his hands and

lathers himself, thinking of the two Nittis. The woman, sometimes unsure, but as often hard-boiled, tough and demanding; and the sensitive child, so easily frightened, so fragile, so
much at the mercy of forces beyond her control.

The unfulfilled promise of Taseen and the Temple haunt-
ed her; but this, Kell thinks, is a good thing. However deep
the wound, it wasn't too late to heal it. The boy's departure
was no abandonment. Nitti had no reason to believe she
didn't deserve Taseen or had proven herself unworthy.

He steps out of the shower and grabs a towel.

The bathroom door is ajar, and through the crack, he sees
Prawan shambling around the bed. Nitti is awake now, standing naked by her vanity with her foot on the stool, spreading
lotion down her leg. Kell watches her doze the white liquid,
acutely conscious of how little he knows about her.

"You needn't bother yourself," Prawan is saying. "I'll send
him on his way."

Kell listens for Nitti's reply, but she's silent.

He wraps the towel around his middle and steps out of
the bathroom.

Prawan lifts her chin, watching him.

Kell meets Nitti's gaze, then he removes the towel, pats
his rear and dries his genitals. Nitti laughs. Prawan acts as if
there is nothing to see. A moment later, she departs to pre-
pare breakfast.

"She's a virgin," Nitti mutters, as if that explains the
housekeeper's harshness.

She faces the window and opens the curtains. Light

washes over her poreless skin, her contoured limbs and the middle without a fold or wrinkle. The vase on her vanity holds a fresh clutch of hibiscus blooms.

Kell tips the vanity's mirror up and regards himself. "You were dreaming last night," he says.

"People dream when they're asleep."

He faces her. "Whatever it was, you were frightened by it."

Nitti turns to her dresser and takes a bra from a drawer.

"How old were you when you married?" she asks.

"We met in college," he says. "I was nineteen."

"How long did it last?"

"Eight years," Kell replies.

"She hurt you." Nitti looks at him.

He nods.

"But you got over it."

"I did."

"So you'll be okay," she says, "if a woman hurts you again."

"No," Kell says. "I won't be okay."

"I'm regretting yesterday," she says softly.

He studies her as she puts the bra on.

"Showing you the Temple," she says. "There's no help in that direction."

She spoke the words simply, and when she looked at him, her eyes were bleak.

"You'll like me better if I stick to my lessons."

"Lessons?"

She nods. "Good ones, from a woman my father knew."

"What did you learn?"

"How to please a man," she says, "without exposing yourself. How to control your feelings, keep them private."

"That's not what I want," he says.

She picks up a blouse. "You don't know what you want."

As changeable as a calotes, Kell thinks. She's turned green, and her crest is bristling. Nitti continues to dress, while he stands there watching, mute and slighted.

She moves past him into the bathroom. He puts his clothes on. When she emerges and seats herself at her vanity, he tries to engage her in conversation: simple things, trivial things that have nothing to do with desire or emotion. Nitti doesn't reply.

Prawan brings them nasi lemak, which they eat from a tray on Nitti's bed. As soon as the meal is done, she returns to her vanity.

He is irrelevant now, as overlooked as a flatworm in a puddle.

When Kell says goodbye, Nitti doesn't turn her head. So he leaves her bedroom on his own and makes his way to the front of the house.

As he enters the octagon he sees Susilo in a morning robe, kissing a woman's hand. She looks in her twenties and is dressed like a Chinese street girl, in a tight silk wrapper and heels.

Kell pauses, uncertain whether to face the old man or return back down the corridor. Before he can decide, the woman moves toward the right-side door and starts down the stair behind a buzzcut boy in motorbike gear.

Susilo closes the door, plants his cane and turns, seeing Kell watching him. Without missing a beat, the old man raises his brows and closes the distance.

"A man must have his pleasures," Susilo smiles with an inevitable look. He slides his arm through Kell's. "Are you leaving us?" He sighs as if he wishes Kell would stay, then he escorts him to the threshold the woman crossed moments before.

"I care about them," Susilo nods, "but they don't care back."

In his eyes, Kell sees a sorrow—something maudlin or tragic. And the sorrow seems shared, as if the old man is comparing their failures.

Susilo opens the door for him and bows. "Please come again soon."

Kell descends the stair, hearing the door close behind him.

He makes his way to his car, seats himself, starts the engine and pulls across the weedy apron.

On the way back to Penang, the sky turns gray. By the time he reaches Taiping, it's raining, and when he crosses the bridge, the downpour is fierce. The pylons and suspension cables ripple through the windshield, and traffic slows to a crawl. On Kell's left, the sea is rafted with fish farms. In a moment of somber reflection, he imagines he's one of the residents. The storm means nothing. He'd been born underwater and spent his life there, senses blunted, confined in his pen. The world above, enormous and far-reaching, was a mystery to him.

3

The return to Jelutong and his work at the Ginger House does little to steady him. His moments of connection with Nitti had been vivid and real—with the ardent frog, in the Nibung delta, among the scrolls on the way to the Temple, hearing her words in the Secret Chamber— She had wanted to be close. The desire to ignore the limits of an "arrangement" was as much hers as his. What had caused her to shut him out?

Had she seen something in him that changed her mind? The barriers between them had collapsed quickly. Was that threatening her? When she'd talked about using her "lessons" to keep him at a distance, it sounded like she was setting the prospect of love aside. He'd imagined they were past that. If they weren't, maybe it was time to let Nitti go, to try and forget her.

An emotional thought, he knows. And an impossible one.

He's been stirred—keenly, intensely—and he's not willing to detach himself from those feelings.

Give her time, he tells himself. It had all happened so quickly. He needed the patience of a transformation technician like the two in his lab. They could sit for hours beneath a steel flow hood, focused, meticulous, peering through the eyepiece of a microscope, probing edited explant tissues with tweezers and needles.

Three days pass, and at the end of the third, Kell sends her a text message. Two days later, he still hasn't heard back.

He buys a note card from the Gardens gift shop, with a drawing of a frog on a branch, and he handwrites a remembrance to her. Their first night together. Her tenderness and depth. He seals the note and sets it on his bedroom dresser. At midnight, geckos invade the room. They climb the walls, whisking and barking, and when dawn finally comes, they're walking upside down on the ceiling.

He showers and dresses and drives to Ipoh. When Prawan opens the door, he hands the envelope to her. She takes it, gives him a mystified look and closes the door in his face without a word.

The drive back to Penang is a long one. Nitti is avoiding him. She must know how he feels. Hurt, puzzled and angry— Is she indifferent?

It's past noon at the Ginger House, and he's in the green mesh enclosure, sweat trickling down his brow. It's hot and humid enough that the white hedychium blooms are releasing their fragrance. Kell's mobile chimes.

It's Yrine, and she's concerned.

"I've never seen her like this," Yrine says. "Whatever happened between you—"

"I didn't do anything," Kell tells her.

"She's locked herself in her room," Yrine explains. "Susilo called me. I went to the house, expecting—" She exhales. "I stood outside her door and knocked and called her name. Finally she spoke to me. She's terribly upset."

Kell tries to imagine her state, to guess at the cause.

"She kept talking about a temple," Yrine says. "I couldn't make sense of it."

Nitti's upset with herself, Kell thinks. Her weakness, her fear. She's upset that she bared her secrets to him and she couldn't unshare them.

"What do you think I should do?" he says.

"Are you going to continue with her?" Yrine asks. Her tone is bleak, as if she thinks it might be better if the relationship ended.

Kell kept silent.

"It doesn't look like it's going to work out," Yrine says.

After an uncomfortable pause, he recounts an affectionate moment with Nitti, speaking more for himself than Yrine. He's like a bittern standing in a river, staring at a wall of jungle, trying to see through it.

When the call ends, Kell's unable to focus on work, so he drives into Georgetown and wanders the streets.

As usual, the traffic is thick, cars barely moving, walkers crowding the shops and stalls. Ice kacang, sauces in bottles, a maze of boxed shoes, worn awnings and bright umbrellas. The colors are jarring and so are the smells: hong bao and dried fish, honeyed meats, pickled fruit soaking in bins.

Tourists in summer dresses jostle past, women of Islam with scarves on their heads, a goateed cornetist playing jazz for change, an old woman squatting on a flattened box with her arms raised. The human market, hatching desires and sating needs, few essential and all of them cheap. How could you live without a glass-beaded purse, an origami fighter jet or a new straw hat?

And then the riot of sound and color fades. A quiet block where the buildings are painted in soft pastels. Jewelry stores line the street, men seated out front with loaded shotguns. Kell wanders into one. A pendant or earrings, he thinks, wondering what Nitti might like. He pauses. What are you doing? he asks himself, still skimming the cases. Buying her a gift seems crazy. He doesn't know if he's going to see her again.

Kell decides on a necklace, a simple gold chain.

It is on his way back to his car that he happens on the carver.

Beneath a white umbrella she's seated, wearing a leather apron, moving a tarnished knife blade over an effigy in wood—a naked female acrobat who'd started a flip and was frozen midair. The acrobat's body looks soft and smooth, almost like flesh. As Kell passes, the carver looks up and her pause triggers his own. She has a serious expression, a gravity that seems out of place in the trifling bazaar. Her eyes are all pupil, her hands netted with seams. Her face had been worked by a master carver, cruelly and deeply.

She passes the naked acrobat to him.

The wood is light, gold with green streaks. Kell holds the acrobat's legs with one hand, turning it, touching its waist with his fingers. "You know your subject."

She doesn't respond. Did she understand what he'd said?

He hands the figurine back to her.

The woman eyes him carefully, as if trying to make up her mind.

Kell turns to leave, but she raises her hand to stop him. She nods at his feet, directing him to remain where he is, and steps into the shadows at the rear of her stall.

She returns a moment later with a wooden mask in her hand. A breath, a squint, then she raises the mask between them, pivoting it, showing one side and the other. It's a female face in pieces: a cheek, the chin, part of the nose, one eye orbit and a curve of brow, all held together with vines and creatures.

She passes it to him.

It's carved from the gold-green wood, Kell sees. The mask is light and its planes are smooth, sculpted with leaves, stitched with frog legs and moth antennae, snake tongues and spider silk. Where the eye should be, a seed capsule grows; and a lizard's tail loop takes an ear lobe's place. One side of the mouth has an uplifted corner that calls Nitti to mind. It's as if the mask can see humor in its own disjointedness.

"Hibiscus," the carver says.

Kell scans the mask's features, looking for a flower; then his thoughts stumble, realizing she's referring to the wood.

Even so, at the word "hibiscus," the shadow of Nitti looms over him; and the consonance seems so unlikely, he imagines for a moment there is some kind of message.

Kell asks the carver for the price, and it's a pittance. So he buys the mask and carries it home, where he hangs it on his bedpost.

Late that night, he is awoken by the chime of his phone.

It's a message from Nitti. "I miss you. Please come."

As he steps toward the house, Prawan waves him to the left stair. Kell had mentioned the stair to Yrine, and he understands now that the housekeeper is expressing her low regard for him. It's the tradition for dwellings with double stairs to have favored guests ascend on the right.

He crosses the threshold and Prawan escorts him to a seat in the guest room.

"She's prettying herself." The housekeeper rolls her tongue, as if there is something she wants to spit out.

Kell sits, expecting her to shuffle away. But she remains standing before him, eyeing him unfavorably. Then she lowers herself onto the chair beside him.

"This valley," she says, "is a safe place. Did you know that? The peaks and knobs protect us from storms."

He raises his brows to her, showing he values the information. She looks like she's been storing up things to get off her chest.

"We're accustomed to having our home used as a brothel," Prawan says.

Kell doesn't reply.

"Susilo never hid his treachery," she says. "His whores served him here, under this roof, then as now. Ibu pretended it wasn't happening. I could not. I was admitting them. And changing his sheets."

"Ibu was Nitti's mother," Kell guesses.

"Ibu *is* Nitti's mother." Prawan's eyes burn. "She's alive, young man."

Then scowling, "She was beautiful once, with all the graces women desire. Now— She has the old smell, the smell of things neglected and forgotten. And her husband's whores come and go, while Nitti has sex with strangers."

The housekeeper pulls a wooden pin out of her hair. "You've joined the outrage." She pushes the pin back in. "Aren't you proud?"

Her hatred is palpable.

"I despise you, Mr. Kell. And so does she," Prawan says. "She knows what you are. She knows Susilo sold Nitti to you. Every sick thing you've done— Ibu knows because I tell her."

With that the housekeeper rises, turns and departs, sandals clapping.

In the wake of this spleen, Kell is motionless, wondering. Nitti had said little about her mother. Was she there, in the house? Susilo was Prawan's employer. He must know how she felt. Had he given her latitude to air her contempt? Maybe the old man believed he'd earned it.

A door opens and Nitti steps forward in a wrinkled blouse and paint-spotted pants. Her hair is down. He stands, searching her eyes, reaching out. She clasps his hand, turns her face and gives him a perfunctory hug. Then she takes a step back, putting space between them.

Her expression is sober, as if she'd been thinking, preparing for something.

"We're going for a walk," she says.

"The Temple?"

"No, downstream. The other way."

She motions and they descend the right stair.

The Chinese gardener is on his knees beside the foundation. As they approach, Kell can see he's using a trowel to clear an overgrown drain.

"This is Kwik," Nitti says.

The gardener looks up, gives Kell a toothless smile, raises his trowel and salutes him with it.

Kell returns the smile. "I'm like you. I work outside."

"He doesn't speak English," Nitti says.

Kwik plants the trowel in the soil and reaches into his pocket. He smiles again, takes Kell's hand and places a dodol in it.

Kell laughs, unwraps the triangular candy and puts it on his tongue. Kwik returns to his work and they continue toward the river.

"We give him food and lodging," Nitti says.

The dodol tastes like toffee.

"Kwik has a crazy nephew," she says. "A rempit, a meth

head. He races his motorbike and runs errands for my father."

"I may have seen him the last time I was here."

Nitti sighs, guessing what that meant.

"Prawan doesn't approve of Susilo's behavior," Kell says. "Or mine either."

"She wants to protect me."

"Do you need protection?" he asks.

Nitti shakes her head as if to say, "You don't understand."

"This place, our home," she slows her steps, "Prawan and my father—" She turns to face him, the depth in her eyes presaging some painful disclosure. "The troubles I've had— I couldn't have survived without them."

She halts, raising her head to gaze at the house's projecting stern, stilted above the slope with the river below.

"The waterside wing," Nitti says. "My mother's in there. Ibu. She had a stroke," she mutters. "She's bedridden, senseless. She doesn't speak."

"That's not what Prawan—"

"I know," Nitti replies. "Prawan loves her. For Prawan, that means imagining Ibu's still a part of our world." She draws a breath. "Kell—"

He watches her, listening, waiting.

"I don't want it to end," she says.

"I don't either," he tells her with feeling.

She shakes her head, searching for words. There are mysteries, things hidden from view— He still knows very little about her.

"We aren't held in high esteem here," she says. "Ibu divided us from our neighbors. Her strangeness, her delusions— My identity card says I'm a Muslim, but it's been many years since I visited a mosque. My father still goes on Fridays to pray. He does what he can to hold us up."

"Are you worried that your family's position will matter to me?"

"No," Nitti says. "But there are things that might."

From a grove of saraca trees, a knocking sounds.

They both turn, seeing two flameback woodpeckers ascending a trunk.

"They're always here," Nitti says, "and always together."

She leads the way down the slope until they reach the path that follows the river. As they step onto it, leaves rain from above. Kell looks up, seeing a tribe of langurs moving through the crowns. A pair of olive-backed sunbirds follows. The bank is tangled with thorny bamboo and mats of vine spilling down. Butterflies—orange cruisers—skim the leafage looking for blooms.

"We're being watched," Nitti says.

A water monitor drifts in the current beside them, a six-foot lizard with all but its head in the flow.

"He knows me," she says.

The reptile forked-tongues the heat, watching Kell with one eye as it shifts its shoulders and crosses the river, heading for the opposite bank.

Farther along, the shoreline trees thicken and the air does too. A hundred paces and the flow slows; and a hundred after that, the surface turns oily and reflective. The river divides, raying into ribbons and torn sheets that wander the mire and darkened soil.

Nitti lets loose of his hand, stepping into a narrow ravine. Water rills through the stilts of small trees rooted there.

"You know these?" She looks down.

Pale green urns crowd the declivity, each with black liquor within.

"I do." He kneels.

Some of the urns are small as thumbs, some bigger than fists, all rubbery—the strangest plants in the jungle. "*Nepenthes ampullaria,*" he says, squeezing the walls of one, touching its mouth.

"Monkey cups," Nitti says.

They eat insects, skinks, frogs by secreting digestive juice. The black fluid within is a soup of dissolved bodies.

"This was Ibu's place," Nitti says. "That's why we're here."

Kell lifts his head. "This ravine?"

"And the swamp beyond."

He rises, seeing urns clustered in the mulch between rills, on the crotches and knees of the dwarfish trees. He grasps a bole. Despite the warm day, its bark is cold.

"Tembusu," he mutters. Ironwood, ancient and hard as prison bars. "Like perfume," he says, "when they're blooming."

She nods. "The wind carries the scent to the veranda."

"In May," Kell says.

She nods again. "The month I was born." Nitti looks downstream, then she reaches for his hand and leads him up out of the declivity.

71

As they continue along the path, the mulch blackens and the pools grow. The tembusu dwindles, replaced by hedges of fern. Nitti's grip tightens.

Nipah palms appear in clumps, trunkless, the large fronds rising straight from the muck. Kell spots some bulbuls in the scrub. Nitti halts on a prominence.

The path has ended. The black waters are all around them, and the air is soupy, damp and pungent. In a place like this, every breath you drew had been used by other creatures.

Why had she brought him here?

"A peat swamp," Kell says. "Swarming with leeches, no doubt."

She nods. "The striped ones follow your steps. If you wade in the water, the buffalo leeches come quickly." Nitti bites her lip and exhales, as if steeling herself to make some important disclosure.

"My childhood was here," she says. "'Keributan.'"

Nitti speaks the name with a bleakness that matches the water's torpor. The stench of mold and rotting duff is rising into Kell's nose.

"The swamp belongs to a snake," Nitti says. "A python, as long as three men. The first time I saw it," she points, "it passed that rock, parted those palms and slid into the water. I was five."

Kell follows the track, wondering if the snake had been watching her as he is now.

"The cicadas were quiet," she says, "and the birds too." She circles her hand around. "I had never heard such silence."

72

Is this why she's brought me here? he thinks. It was more than the drama of her telling. She was sharing some kind of secret.

"The next time," she says, "it was coiled there, in the ferns with the sun on its back."

Even in Nitti's most revealed moments, Kell thinks, there had been things hidden.

"I could see the patterns," she says, "on its scaly back. The black and amber reticulations. Its blue iridescence."

"And again, before I left for the States," Nitti points upstream, "I saw it winding through the ironwood and the monkey cups. I was ten feet away. It could have swallowed me whole."

There is fear in her voice, a shrinking candor. And Kell sees fear in her eyes, but there is courage as well. She wants to trust me, he thinks. To rely on me.

"It's still here," Nitti says.

She doesn't look, but he does, scanning the marsh around them. The growth is dry in spots. You would hear a rustling, he thinks. Or you'd spot its long head sliding through the reeds, eye blazing with sun, the forked tongue snipping out.

"I saw one feeding at the Zoo Negara," he says, "when I first arrived."

"It coils around its victim," she says, "binds its chest—"

"They squeeze," he nods, "until they've stopped the prey's breath."

Nitti is staring at him.

"The jaws open wide," she says softly, "five times as wide

as its body. Five times." Her lip snags. "Its head slides over you like a giant sock, and then you're inside."

Nitti inhales slowly, deeply, as if bracing herself.

"That's my dream," she confesses. "The one I always have. The one I had the night before you left. I'm sorry I pushed you away."

Kell accepts her words in the quiet, remembering. Trying to imagine.

"In my dream, there's a storm," she says. "It churns the black waters. Waves become walls, steep walls that curl and crash into each other. The giant python waits on the shore, coiled on the bough of a naked tree, orange eyes watching."

"How long has this—"

"The past is my enemy," she says. "I can't allow it to steal my life."

"Can the past do that?"

"It can," she murmurs. Then she straightens herself. "Keributan," she says, scanning the swamp. "Poison in the monkey cups, leeches in the pools. The leaves fall and join the decay."

On the return, Kell is silent.

As they pass the spot where the swamp begins, he notices a tall nyatoh with a long-legged huntsman on it, arms spread over the rough bark. Like a warning not to return, or of some contagion or infection received.

Once the swamp has vanished from view, Kell stops beside a banana thicket.

"I want you to know," he clasps Nitti's arm. "I'm not afraid of things that have pained or frightened you. Honesty will only make us stronger."

Nitti sighs and touches his cheek.

He reaches into his pants pocket and draws out a small white box. "For the future," he says, and he hands it to her.

She opens the lid, sees the gold chain and lifts it out.

Kell fastens it around her neck, saying something about the chain protecting her heart from troubling thoughts.

Then they continue down the path, sun bright and the river as well.

As they approach Nitti's home, Kell notices some oddities in its upkeep. In front the stilts are clear, but facing the river, they're bound with vines. In places, the vines have reached the walls and wandered across them. A breeze lifts the leaves and swings the tails. Hasn't the gardener noticed the encroachment?

Kell sees a small fig tree rooted on a windowsill of the waterside wing. And when he looks at the pane, he sees a silhouette on the drape. A woman—one with stooped shoulders and her hair bound up at the rear. Her profile thins magically, ghostlike. She's turned, she's raising one arm— The drape shifts. Is she peering out at them?

"Ibu," he murmurs, glancing at Nitti.

"No," she says with alarm. "That's Prawan."

Kell nods, but slowly, unsurely.

Nitti seems troubled, distracted, as if she is unsure herself.

On their way back from the swamp, it had seemed to Kell that Nitti's sharing of her childhood fears was stringing a new bridge between them. But by the time they enter the house, she seems dispirited, exhausted or disturbed by something malign.

She retreats to her bedroom and lies down. Kell goes looking for Susilo.

He is seated on the veranda with a glass of tea in his hand.

Kell pulls a chair closer and sits beside him.

Minutes pass without either saying a word. Then Kell wades in.

"In the States," he says, "when someone acts or speaks without thinking of others, we say they're 'taking liberties.'"

"I know the expression," Susilo replies.

"For a housekeeper, Prawan takes liberties."

Susilo sips his tea. Kell isn't sure if he's going to answer.

Finally, the old man speaks. "Nitti cares for you," he says.

"And I care for her," Kell replies.

"Her fondness," Susilo goes on, "upsets her. Her hopes have raised some fears." He pauses, holding his words back. "It's normal for a father to worry about his daughter."

Susilo's tone and the wear in his eyes hint at a long disquiet.

"You're Nitti's good fortune. I believe that now," the old man says. "And because you're close and are growing closer, it's time that I share some things with you. Unpleasant things." He frowns at his tea.

"Nitti told me about Ibu's stroke," Kell says, "and how her neglect of Islam isolated you from your neighbors."

"Our family has been through difficult times." Susilo looks toward the river. "My wife was ill. Ill in her mind. Before the stroke."

He sets his tea on the table beside him.

"She lived in a world of her own. When we first met, I was attracted by that. Her exaggerations, her fantasies. She performed in amateur dramas. She thought she would be a great actress. She imagined sharing the stage with a star of the day, and she talked about having an affair with him, even though they were strangers.

"I went along with this. 'It's harmless,' I thought. 'She's a rare creature.'

"My view of things changed with her disappearances. I'd go to her room in the evening, and it would be empty. Prawan knew where she was. It was only by accident—"

He shifted his gaze toward the swamp.

"Through the dining room window, I saw a torch in the darkness down there. I waited up and confronted her. She didn't care that I knew." Susilo bowed his head. "I was still in love with her."

"What was she doing?" Kell asks.

"Our imam would've called it heresy. I did what I could to keep it secret. Her nightly visits to Keributan—the name she gave the place—seemed to connect her to spiritual things, to give her a comfort she needed."

A shiver climbs Kell's neck.

"It isn't just 'isolation,'" Susilo says. "We have laws against these kinds of things. She could have been arrested." He faces

Kell, pained, squinting. "Things turned ominous quickly. She would return bleary-eyed with her clothing soaked, her face scratched by thorns, leeches hanging from her legs. There was a place she bathed and a gathering of creatures and forces only she understood."

Kell pictures a woman in water to her waist, the black swamp circled around her, silvered by the moon. "Prawan was a part of this?"

Susilo nods. "She was wedded to Ibu's madness. She still is."

A cicada sounds like a braking railroad wheel, metallic and shrill.

"Except for Prawan," the old man says, "my wife was alone. The people around her were ghosts that came and went, appearing through the fog and sinking back into it. She began to judge us, to make demands. Small things at first—rules, taboos. Foods that couldn't be eaten, words that couldn't be spoken.

"People suspected. When Ibu was out in public, there was no hiding her strange state. I did what I could to preserve our privacy."

It's a jarring picture for Kell.

"The pregnancy," Susilo says, "seemed cause for hope. I thought motherhood might bring my wife back. But she was already lost. Nitti became part of Ibu's delusion—before she was born. My wife believed the infant was her companion in her nightly rites. Then the discomforts came, and as they mounted, so did her protests."

Susilo pauses and draws a breath. When he resumes, his voice is trammeled with grief. "She thought something foul was growing inside her."

He craned at Kell over the arm of his chair.

"If you care for my daughter," Susilo says, "you must understand how Ibu's fantasies would affect a child. They were frightening to Nitti. Terrifying."

It's hard for Kell to imagine.

Silence except for the river's sigh.

"Ibu is in the waterside wing," Kell says.

"She is."

"You visit her."

Susilo shakes his head. "Kwik and I take flowers from the garden and put them beneath her window."

He was acting as if his wife was already dead.

"Considering how things turned out, you might think she had the powers she claimed. I'm Nitti's guardian now. But this house and the land it sits on was deeded to Ibu, and she passed control to Prawan in the event of her death or disablement.

"So," Susilo downs the last of his tea, "it's Prawan's home now."

The information surprises Kell.

The old man looks across the river, into the jungle.

Not the trunk of his family tree, Kell thinks. Or even a branch. Nitti's father was an epiphyte rooted in a vee, living on dew.

Kell returns to Nitti's room to find her stretched on the bed.

She opens her eyes, sees him, smiles and reaches out her hand. He sits beside her.

"You like what you do," she says, "at the Gardens."

"Very much."

"There's a feeling of power," she guesses.

"And powerlessness," he says.

"When the gingers don't change as you wish."

"That's right."

"You cut their old genes," she snips two fingers, "and add new ones."

"Something like that."

"You have to know what you're doing," she says.

Kell nods.

"Could you change me that way?"

He laughs. "I may like you the way you are."

"May?"

He's silent, waiting for her thought to pass.

"What if I asked you to?" she says. "How would you do it? Where would you cut?" Nitti touches her sternum. "My heart. My head—" She tips her crown toward him.

He puts his hand to her ear, feeling the fine strands by her temple.

"Would it hurt?" she says.

"It might," he replies, "depending on what you asked me to change."

The latch clicks. Kell turns his head.

The door swings open and Prawan steps forward, silver tray in her hand. She avoids looking at either of them, sets the tray on the bed, removes the jar from the vanity drawer and shakes out a pill. She passes it to Nitti along with a glass of water.

The housekeeper's hand dips into her apron pocket and emerges with an object. She places it on the vanity counter beside the rubber goose and slips the medication back in the drawer. Then, as quietly as she entered, Prawan departs.

Nitti puts the pill on her tongue and washes it down.

"What do those do?" Kell asks.

"They calm me." She speaks without looking up.

The new object on the bedstand, Kell sees, is an empty perfume bottle of amethyst glass. He reaches for it, lifting it by its atomizer bulb.

"I played with that," Nitti says, "when I was a child."

"The toys please you?"

Nitti shakes her head. "Prawan thinks the memories will—"

"Will what?"

"Draw us together. Ibu and I."

"Prawan wants that?" he says.

Nitti nods.

"What about you?"

"Oh no," she shakes her head. "That will never happen—"

Her voice is unnaturally high, and her eyes are a child's. There's a hint of pleading in them.

He wants to help her, whatever help means. But what can he do? The memory of an intimate smile—tender, wistful, the promise of safety and bliss—lived in his heart. He could bring it to mind any time he wished. His mother, his Ibu, was the sun that shone over him, no matter how far he roamed. That's what he knew about the roots of love. Nothing more than that.

Nitti's strange mother, a defeated ayah, the imperious Prawan— What Kell had learned was already too much. It exceeded his understanding. If he knew more, would he develop convictions, answers? As a partner— Could he ever be any use to Nitti?

"It will be hard," he says, "but I'm going to try."

Nitti regards him.

"To give you whatever help I can," he says. "I'm in love with you, Nitti."

She clasps his wrist and bows her head.

"Will you trust me?" he asks.

She nods.

Kell faces the armoire and opens the door. "Take me for a walk," he says, "down the waterside wing."

She's as still as a cat gecko frozen on a leaf.

"Nitti—"

"I'd rather not."

"We're close in many ways," Kell says, "but in others, I feel like I barely know you."

"Please," she whispers.

"I need to know about this," he says gently, "don't I?"

His question hangs in the air between them. Finally, she nods.

As Kell retrieves some clothing for her, she sighs and rises like a child called to a task. He helps her dress and they leave her room, starting along the well-lit corridor.

"When was the last time you saw her?" he asks.

"I was sixteen."

"The place where she stays— She's been there the whole time?"

Nitti nods. "Ayah sleeps alone. When I returned from the States, I took my old room."

"Prawan cares for her," he says.

Nitti nods. "Prawan makes special food and brings it to her. Prawan washes her. Prawan takes her clothes off and puts them on."

"Special food?"

"The same as before," Nitti says. "Prawan tells us everything." Then softly, "I don't want to know."

They pass through the empty dining area. Through the window, Kell sees a leaning fence crowned with beaumontia. The twisting vine was dragging it down.

"Ibu never leaves?" he asks. "Prawan never escorts her out?"

"Never," Nitti says.

"I'm trying to picture her, before the stroke."

His attempt to summon an image unsettles Nitti. She is trusting him, and the trust is taking courage.

83

"She was taller than I am. Her hair was clipped short. She preferred men's clothes. Prawan searched the markets for them. Ibu liked to look at herself in the mirror—a tall mirror beside her bed. Sometimes she'd be an actress, posing in it, raising her arms, speaking her lines."

"You were with her?"

Nitti nods. "When she let me."

The entrance to the waterside wing comes into view. Nitti slows. Kell can feel her reluctance.

"I'm listening," Kell says. "You were with her, in her room."

"Prawan made up her face," Nitti says.

He can hear the agitation in her voice.

"How did she make it up?" Kell asks.

Nitti shakes her head.

"She wasn't trying to be attractive."

"No," Nitti says.

They reach the turn and make it together. The hall down the waterside wing is visible now, a lone door at the end on the left.

"Tell me about the stroke."

"She was bathing," Nitti says. "Prawan was with her."

"What did it do, physically?"

"Twisted her spine," Nitti answers. "Froze her arm."

"She can't speak?"

"Not a word," she whispers.

An old woman, Kell thinks, crippled, bedridden, left to the care of a crazy housekeeper who's dripping poison into her charge's ear.

84

Closer and closer they draw to Ibu's sanctum. The edge of fear in Nitti's eyes sharpens with every step.

"I wasn't the child she wanted," she says.

He's gripping her hand, coaxing her forward.

"She used Keributan to threaten you," he says.

Nitti bows her head.

Was she hiding her face, ashamed or afraid— Kell couldn't tell.

"It's more than a place in the peat swamp," he says.

"Keributan," Nitti answers, "is the dark water beneath us."

"I don't understand."

"We're suspended above it," Nitti says. "All of us. We're at Ibu's mercy: she can hold on to us, or she can let go."

Her fearful words echo down the dimly lit passage, joining their muted footsteps and uneven breath. Elsewhere the house is tiled, but here the floor is wooden and damp. A briny stench rises from the planks.

"She brought back sludge in a jar," Nitti says, "and salved herself with it. The smell of Keributan was everywhere."

Kell sees her nose twitch. Can she smell the swamp even now?

The door looms closer. Nitti stares at the knob as if she thinks it's about to open.

She halts. Her head ticks, hearing noises or voices. All at once she's shivering, shaking uncontrollably, chest heaving as if she can't breathe.

Kell circles her shoulders with his arm, swinging her around, escorting her back down the hall.

It isn't until they've rounded the corner and the waterside wing is out of sight that Nitti's heaving fades. Clarity reappears in her eyes. She blinks, and her tongue wets her lower lip.

"It's always with you," Kell says softly.

"Always," she sighs.

With that sigh, it was as if an awful secret had passed into the world.

He knows more now, but the knowledge had come at a price. He'd pushed her too hard. They sit in the guest room for an hour, then Kell suggests they go outside. He wants to get her away from the house.

They cross the river and climb a rise. With his new awareness, the relationship is evolving in ways he would not have foreseen. He's closer to Nitti, more conscious of the threats she feels. At the same time, there's a new distance between them, as if what he'd learned demanded, for her, a new kind of self-protection.

She was more vulnerable now. And part of her had gone into hiding.

A grove of borassodendron palms rises ahead, roofing the sky with bushy sprays. They wander beneath, not holding hands, not speaking. Filmy ferns, jewel bugs and selaginella, branching and blue. A scatch of woodshrikes, the whir of cicadas— All the wild things he knows so well. But Nitti is an enigma, a maze to which he is not admitted. His heart wants to retract like a snail shrinking into its shell, but he won't let it. He'd asked for her trust, and he's going to earn it.

By the time they head back, a gray light has settled, a twilight before twilight's time. Kell had planned to spend the night with her and return to Penang the following morning. Prawan serves a light dinner, and they return to Nitti's room.

As soon as she's closed the door, Nitti begins to undress.

Once she's naked, she turns to him, removing his belt, unbuttoning his shirt.

Nitti settles him on the bed, palming his chest, hiding her eyes.

She swipes a match, and a bead of fire appears at its end. She lights the wick of a beeswax taper, and with its shadows wavering over her, she stretches beside him.

Kell kisses her lips. His hand feathers her back, a mitt-shaped macaranga leaf idling in the breeze. He feels her tongue on his cheek.

Then Nitti stands on her knees and folds his head in her arms. Kell's heart is sluggish, but he returns the affection, using both hands to squeeze her waist.

Is it me? he thinks. Where is the desire that usually surfaced so easily?

Her lips cross his brow, nipping his lid, steaming his ear. Her thighs clench one of his, like a hammerhead worm cornering prey, leaving slimy secretions. Kell's hand divides her rear, an army of ants descending into a glade.

"You're distracted," she says.

He thinks, Maybe I am.

She hurries ahead, attacking his groin with her hands and mouth, like a pangolin tearing open a termite mound. He raises himself, watching her bob in the strobing light. It's shadow puppetry, done for laughs, like a flameback pecking grubs from a branch. The jungle images are reflexive and unthinking.

Kell takes her face in his hands and lifts it. Her features shift with the flicker. Puzzling brows, an uncertain lip—

Had it always been there? He hadn't noticed it before. A jagged line at the corner of Nitti's eye. Was it a scar or a mark she'd carried from birth?

He puts the tip of his finger on it. "Were you hurt?"

Nitti turns her head. "Don't."

He pinches her chin, moving her face back to where it was.

But what he has learned taints his view: he is seeing her now in two dimensions. There's a living child, treasured and safe in the Secret Chamber; and there is one half-dead, bereft and alone, sinking into the waters of Keributan.

What does he know of this strange creature?

Who is the real Nitti?

There's a guise, a mask. For the first time, Kell can see it.

Does he love her? Yes, oh yes—certainly yes. Why can't he feel it?

He can see the side of her nose, straight and poreless; the corner of her mouth, blissful and untormented. And through the carved leafage, a lock of unbraided hair hangs wavy and fine. But her cheeks, while smooth, are no longer soft and yielding; they're stiff and grained. One eye is a seedpod, immobile. The other is hers. Nitti's dark eye, guileless and true, ever and always, rapt at times, at others so fearless it swallows your own—

That eye is fixed on him now, peering through the orbit of the wooden mask, wondering.

4

Kell arrives at his home in Jelutong at half past ten the next morning.

He takes his overnight bag from the trunk of his car, enters through the kitchen and climbs the stair. In the bedroom he sets his bag on the mattress and unzips it, removing a handful of clothes. Then he pauses and peers at the carved face.

He drops the clothes and steps toward the mask. He places his thumb on the wooden chin, curling his fingers around the edge of the cheek, lifting the light object, removing it from the bedpost.

Kell turns the face in his hands, feeling its thinness behind the half-shell eye, the beak prick and swept wing of the bird by its ear, the groove at the brow where the flesh turns to leaves. He remembers the maker's expression, her seamed palms and the moment she said "hibiscus." He thinks about

Nitti, her secrets, her doubts, her terrors and the need to hide them. And he thinks about his struggle to feel close to her the previous night.

Kell sits on the bed.

Her mask, he thought. How long had she worn it?

From the day she first felt her mother's hatred, he thinks. From the day she'd been threatened by Keributan. It was fear. Fear was the carver.

The wood in his hands is stiff and unfeeling. A lifeless thing, Kell thinks. How much of Nitti's warmth and care had flowed into the mask she wore? How much of her spirit, over how many years?

She had needed the mask to protect herself. But she was wearing it now with him.

He gazes through the empty eyehole, then he draws a breath and returns the carved face to the bedpost. It was more than an omen, he thinks. It's a curse that has to be overcome.

Kell is in the Ginger House lab helping a female post-doc culture *Agrobacterium*. A predacious microbe, *Agro* is the change agent for plants, the only one like it known to science.

From a shelved rack full of petri dishes, Kell and the post-doc each take two and move them to a rotating shaker table. Then two more and two more, while the shaker sloshes the dollop of earth-brown mash in each dish. The brown *Agro* will attack a plant's tissue, invade it and so thoroughly assault its identity that the plant's genome is altered.

Kell checks the ringer of his phone, making sure it is on. Then he continues to help the post-doc transfer petri dishes to the shaker.

Altering the makeup of gingers wasn't easy. Most of the edits were disappointments, and the breakthroughs were all hard-earned. But losses were measured in time and dollars. They were plants; you could always grow more, and the mistakes didn't matter.

Kell's thoughts return to Nitti.

She's important to him, very important. Keeping their love alive means open hearts, shorn of defenses. Surely she knows she has no cause for fear, no reason to protect herself—not from him. But amid this protestation, Kell is apprehensive about what it will take to make Nitti feel safe. He had so little understanding of her private thoughts and feelings. Visiting the waterside wing had been a foolish mistake; and unlike those in the lab, mistakes with someone you care for have consequences.

What could he do? What kind of operation would edit out fear and replace it with trust?

For a moment, he amuses himself, imagining he's refashioned Nitti as she'd requested. His theorized edits had all been made. The *Agro* was purged before it could destroy its prey. His love is a thriving explant now, crowding her incubation chamber, ready to spread her branches and leaf out in the sun. The elements are in her favor. The one she loves is posted nearby, and he's sworn to protect her.

Ten minutes later, he is headed for Ipoh. As he passes through Taiping, he gets a text from her. She's taking a nap. Prawan will let him in.

The housekeeper leads him down the corridor. He enters Nitti's room and closes the door behind him. She's asleep on the coverlet. Nitti has a blouse on, but her legs are bare. A beam of light from a gap in the curtains glosses her naked hip.

Kell stretches beside her, clothed. He puts his hand on her waist and moves it around her haunch, feeling the smooth parabola made taut by her bent knee. His desire has returned—that special fusion of ardor and uncertainty—so melting, so potent. Her mystery was an aphrodisiac. But it was an impediment too, and their future depended on its removal.

He allows himself to imagine Nitti transformed. Nitti maskless, with her needs exposed and her love pouring out. A fantasy, is it? Believing in her, Kell thinks, is a moral act, an expression of hope.

"Nitti," he whispers.

His palm caresses her thigh, so perfectly sleek.

Her lids part, her eyes dark; her lips offer themselves, perfectly willing.

He kisses her, thinking of the secrets inside her still undisclosed, the sighs, the pain, the crying words not yet spoken.

"I want us to be permanent," he says.

"Permanent."

"I want to fall asleep with you every night, and wake up with you every morning."

She raises her hands. Her eyes are close, so close it seems they are inside his head. Nitti kisses his ear. He feels her warm breath on his cheek.

She'd be safe with him, he thinks. Whatever fears she had, she would confide them, knowing he would understand. If things were distressing for her, they'd retreat together. He'd be there beside her in the Secret Chamber, listening to the words of the forlorn child, giving her comfort and strength until she was ready to return to the world.

"Will you trust me?" he says.

"I will."

"There's a part of you that's frightened." Kell speaks softly, tenderly, with great concern for her feelings. "A part of you that's hidden."

"I know." Nitti's voice is small.

"You don't have to protect yourself—"

Her face is expressionless now.

"I'll keep you safe," Kell says.

He touches her temple.

"Have I done something wrong?" she says in a little girl's voice.

Kell sighs. Then he whispers, "You have."

Silence.

As gently as he can, he says, "You've been wearing a mask. With me."

Her fingers have frozen on his chest. Kell can feel them trembling. There's a halt in her breath.

"If there are things I don't know," he says, "I want you to tell me."

Her shoulder rotates against his chest as if she means to turn away. He's aware in a heartbeat of the old house, Prawan, this room, Susilo and the many things Nitti might like to bury. Kell puts his arm around her, trying to halt her retreat.

"That will be hard," she says, her voice breaking.

"Please," Kell says.

"I don't want to lose you," Nitti sobs.

"You won't, I swear—" He kisses her cheeks alternately as he speaks. "You won't, you won't—"

"Are you sure?"

"If I have doubts," he says, "I'm not going to listen to them. I've never cared this much about anyone. Tell me you understand what I'm saying."

Nitti's lips part. She swallows.

Then her head bows. She shudders and presses her cheek to his shoulder.

"I do," she whimpers. "I do."

They are naked together all that afternoon. Kell does everything he can to make Nitti feel his desire and affection. Her raw emotions had never been so visible or open to him. They were like the unrolling leaves of a bird's nest fern, radiating from her heart in all directions. The two were side by side at first, then she straddled him, then he was behind her, holding her waist. The flirtation was gone—the crooked smile, her glittering eyes, the dodge and baffle around something hidden. The spotty shows of command vanished as well, replaced by effusions that drew them closer.

As for the mask— Another woman, most others perhaps, would have taken his request amiss. Who could admit to deception? Nitti might have been indignant, defended her guise as camouflage, like the leafy armor of a horned frog. "This is me," she might have said. "It can't be removed."

But she didn't deny the disguise. Nitti knew. She lived with the sadness and guilt that came with hiding her real state from him and everyone else. Was the truth so grim, so unnegotiable? As much as she'd told him about herself, it was hard to understand what had driven her need for that kind of privacy.

In the strokes and caresses, the noises and clutching, all signs of reserve seemed to vanish. What can you see of a partner in passion—a shocking gravity, the immovable stare, her glad receipt of oblivion? Truth declares itself between gasps. Love comes first, Kell thought. The answers that he waited on, and needed, would come later.

After what must have been hours, the frenzy subsided.

They remained entwined, sweating and close, limbs folded together. As their breathing slowed, their limbs shifted, finding their way below and around each other like wandering roots. Gliding hands, mossy hair; the muscled skin is dew damp, and the slots between are slippery as white jelly fungus.

With the passage of time, they stretch out on their backs, side by side on a bed surrounded by jungle. A ceiling of mist hangs low, laden with chips of green. Lianas serpent the muzz, and boles of red meranti pierce it. A flock of leafbirds, like a puff of verdure, is blowing from tree to tree.

After minutes or hours, the light through the patterned curtains has plaited their legs, as if they'd grown over with wild pepper. Now? he thinks. Was this the time?

Kell allows himself to pretend that he and Nitti are in the Secret Chamber, far from the world, hidden from view.

"I want to know—" He begins slowly, trying to remove from his voice any hint of emotion. "About Keributan."

Nitti shivers.

Kell lets a moment pass. He raises his hand and sets it on hers.

"And the python," he says. "I want to know how it got into your dreams."

She exhales, it seems, with relief. She wants him to share her distress. She's vulnerable, he thinks. Has she put the mask aside? Is she shifting it now, or still behind it?

"I'm listening," he says.

He's like a turtle circling a fig tree, waiting for the fruit to drop.

"It doesn't have arms or legs," Nitti says, like a child seeing the creature for the very first time. Her voice catches. She shakes her head. "I can't—"

"You can," he replies. "I love you, Nitti. For me, you can."

98

She takes a breath. "It's a tube," she says. "A tube of muscle. Crooked, on the ground, cold to touch. It feels me with its belly: when I move, the ground trembles; no matter how slowly I move or how softly, it feels my steps. It's smart. Much smarter than I am."

"Its home is in Keributan. Is that right?"

"Yes."

"It's late afternoon," Kell says. "Where is it now? Right now."

"I don't know."

"It's not here in your room. It's not in the house. Is it?"

"No," she says. "Not in the daytime. It's in the jungle. Descending a slope, straight as a log. Crawling through a trench in the swamp. Sipping black water. Listening, tasting the air with its tongue."

"It's by accident," he says, "that you see it. When you're down by the river."

"That's right. By accident. It knows how to hide itself."

"Things are different at night," Kell guesses.

"Yes."

"What happens then?"

"Please, don't ask me," she implores him.

"It isn't real, Nitti. It's all in your mind."

"Even so—"

"If a fear isn't real," he says, "why should it frighten us?"

She's silent.

"Where is the python at night?" he says gently. "Is it here in the house?"

"Sometimes."

"Where?"

"With Ibu. In the hall outside Ayah's room. Under the dining room table."

"What is it doing?" he asks.

Silence, and then— "It's thinking of me. It's seeing me through the walls. It's smelling my hair."

"Does it come here? Is it in your room?"

"At night it is. It's on the floor beside my bed, coiled like a giant stump, with its head on top. Its eyes are watching and its tongue flicks out. Beneath its scaly skin I can see the knobs of its spine. It hasn't eaten for months."

"You're dreaming this?" he asks. "Or are you awake, imagining it?"

"I'm not sure."

"You're afraid the python is going to attack you."

"No."

"Tell me," he says.

"It wants me to come with it to Keributan," Nitti says.

Kell slides his arm beneath her back. She feels soft and limp.

"What happens next," he asks.

"I do as it says." Nitti starts to cry.

"I'm here," he reminds her. He can feel her helplessness and her self-pity. She'd lived with this nightmare for a long time.

What could be stranger, Kell thinks, than to find a dream snake between yourself and the woman you love. Nitti is sobbing as if they had launched on a perilous crossing. Or worse:

that her fear was a place he could never reach. A moat had opened between them, and the black waters were churning there. She was on an island circled by Keributan.

"What happens next?" he asks again.

"Kell," she sobs, "I can't."

"You're following the snake," he says. "I'm here. I'm on the path with you. The python is leading us into the swamp."

Silence.

Nitti is shaking like a little bronze cuckoo in a thunderstorm. At first Kell thinks it's fear; then all at once, it's a spasm of yielding.

A child's laugh flies from her lips.

I'm asleep, Kell thinks. After the long bout of love, he'd nodded off.

Nitti was a child again, and so was he.

She shivers, she gasps. Then a sigh, a trigger, and all at once a cloudburst is overhead. I'm dreaming, Kell thinks, or the dream is Nitti's and he is somehow in it.

Drops of black are falling on the leaves around them, dotting Nitti's hair and—when she turns to face him—her cheeks and brow. She's a young girl, and he's a boy, but they aren't in the Secret Chamber together. It's past midnight, and they're on the path beside the river, with the giant python gliding ahead.

It's raining Keributan.

Nitti squints at the spatter. Her nostrils flare at the tarry smell.

The python's thick body is dotted too, winding up an

incline, skirting a boulder, descending toward the oily swamp that the cloudburst feeds. Kell can see the cobbled shore now, and the quiet black water stretching to either side.

The snake has halted. Its head circles, turning to fix on Nitti. It cares not a whit about him.

Nitti is motionless, watching as the snake's head looms closer, as large as hers.

Apricot eyes with vertical slits, tongue white-tipped and flicking, smelling her state. Its head freezes while it pulls its body forward, kinking its neck for the strike.

Nitti is mesmerized. The python can hear her thoughts.

She'll be struck, Kell sees. She'll be bound tight. And the python will spread its jaws to consume her.

Nitti cries out. Her arm flails, stirring the dream. Or is he still in it?

Through the darkness, Kell sees her hand catch the vase on the bedstand. He hears it fall, shattering; and lurching up, he sees the hibiscus blooms dashed across the pavers.

He's in the dimly lit room, Kell thinks.

But Nitti is still asleep, still on the path. "Please," she begs him. Or is she addressing the python? "Please, please—"

Kell has no way of interpreting her desperate appeal. But the submission in her voice, the look in her eye—

She's surrendering to the snake, confessing that her love for Kell is a terrible mistake, as if by renouncing it her terror will end.

No, no, no, he thinks. But he can't reach her, and the snake doesn't care.

The rain of Keributan is falling harder, drowning the hills, filling the river, covering everything with its gleaming black. Waves are crossing the growing lake, a vast monkey cup of dissolving parts, a poisonous stew into which all life on earth will be cast.

Nitti wraps her arms around herself, knowing she'll be first.

What happens next, Kell could not have imagined—like a jungle moment when a frenzied insect flies under your nose, and the instant it lands it turns into a twig.

Nitti stiffens and her face goes blank.

Kell grasps her shoulders. "It's alright," he says.

A twisted bedsheet binds her arm. The ceiling fan is turning, and the reflected blades strobe in her eyes.

"Nitti?"

She seems not to hear him. Sweat beads her brow, but her features are smooth, slack, flawless.

"Nitti," Kell insists.

Blank, neither woman nor child, her face is as fixed as a wooden mask.

Kell rises, puts his feet on the pavers, avoiding the shards of the broken vase, and flings the door open. Then he's shouting as loud as he can for help.

The doctor comes and stays through the late hours, preaching calm. He argues against moving Nitti to the hospital until the following day. And his advice proves wise, as her lucidity returns by degrees with Susilo's help.

The old man remained by the bed, holding his daughter's hand, speaking in a gentle, reassuring voice. For hours, there was only the black swamp with a scarlet hibiscus floating on its surface.

Susilo showed what seemed to Kell an unusual calm amid his devastation. What was missing from his reaction was shock. Prawan's behavior, too, was hard to understand. There was an element, Kell thought, of acceptance.

Gradually Susilo brought his daughter back. By midnight, she was able to identify everyone in the room. Kell stood by the vanity, remembering what Susilo had told him about the fears his daughter experienced as a child. Prawan sat silent on the other side of the bed. She blamed Kell for what had happened, and she made no effort to hide her contempt.

"He's endangering her," she told Susilo. "He understands nothing."

Kell didn't reply. What could he say?

At 4 a.m., Susilo kisses his daughter and returns to his room. Kwik escorts the doctor out, while Prawan and Kell tend to the patient. Does she want to talk? Is she hungry? Does she feel like sleeping? The housekeeper refuses to leave Kell alone with her. When Nitti drops off, he stretches out on the floor of the guest room.

It's near noon when he wakes. He returns to her bedroom to find her in bed, sitting with a pillow behind her back. Prawan is there with buns and tea. Nitti eyes him over the housekeeper's shoulder.

"This is not your best." Prawan reaches to straighten Nitti's hair.

"Would you like to talk?" Kell asks.

Prawan glares at him. "You're the problem here."

Nitti seems to absorb the housekeeper's words. Kell struggles to answer the accusation.

"You don't have any idea what's happened," Prawan says. "Do you."

It's true, Kell thinks. He has no idea.

"You've done her harm, Mr. Kell," Prawan says. "And if you remain, more harm will come."

Nitti's gaze narrows, as if she's having trouble seeing him or is seeing him now with different eyes.

"We want you to leave," Prawan says.

Who is she speaking for? Kell thinks.

Prawan turns her cheek and retrieves her tray, falling back into her servile role. Without another word she leaves the room, closing the door behind her.

Kell steps toward the bed. He smiles at Nitti and raises his hand to her shoulder.

Nitti recoils. She draws her knees up and clasps her arms around them. Before he can speak, she begins to cry. Kell stands motionless, watching.

"Would you like me to—"

She shakes her head, not wanting to hear.

Susilo enters the room and canes closer, stopping beside his daughter. He looks from Nitti to Kell, feeling the tension, seeing the deadlock.

"I want to stay with her," Kell says.

Susilo sighs. "It's really best that you leave."

"Are you sure?"

Susilo purses his lips and nods.

So, reluctantly, Kell departs.

He's passing through the mountains making for Taiping when the clouds erupt and the rains come down. His wipers can't clear the flood, so he slows and creeps cautiously forward. Out of the downpour a siren rises, and through the blurred windshield he sees the flashing lights of an emergency van.

An accident or ill health— A stranger in peril.

And the woman in the house by the river— She's in peril too. And she too seems like a stranger.

Alone in his bedroom in Jelutong, heralds of woe invade Kell's sleep. The house geckos bark to fend off cannibal roommates. Mosquitoes sing of malaria and dengue. A cat infected with encephalitis yowls below his window. And the prayers, the prayers won't stop. Seven neighborhood mosques broadcast together, chanting warnings and forbidding laments.

Then the giant python finds a cleft in his dream and glides into it.

The sky is spectral, livid and apocalyptic. A crescent moon cuts through a ceiling of cloud. He's standing on the rise overlooking the peat swamp. Beyond the pools, a ravine is banked with polygon ferns, lush and damp, tangled and close— And at the ravine's mouth, the ferns are shifting.

As Kell watches, a scaly nose appears. The snake's giant head pushes out, orange eyes glaring, its tongue flicking and sensing.

The python is winding through the pools, dipping beneath the dark water and gliding out, its body in sections that stretch and compress. Then it reaches mud, it's gliding and whole again, the black and amber reticulations flexing as it moves. Facets of fear, windows of doom—

As Kell turns to follow its path, a great sea appears, black to the far horizon. Its surface is crossed by parallel ripples, and in that unflagging movement he senses the nature of Keributan—unrelenting, hateful of life. The shore is a slope of gray cobbles, and on that slope a leafless tree stands, naked and bleached.

The giant python is winding over the cobbles. It reaches the tree, anchors its tail, winds itself around the trunk and coils up it.

"The snake will wait," a voice says.

For what? he wonders.

"For me," the voice says.

Nitti is standing on the rise beside him, facing the sea. She's wearing the hibiscus mask.

The python reaches a projecting branch and gathers itself on it. Its head turns, eyes on Nitti. The carved leaves of the mask cover her temple. Her ear is a fungus shell, and a small wooden bird is poised over her brow, its sharp bill dividing it.

She's not a child, he thinks. And she's no fool.

What protection did she imagine the mask gave her?

The next morning, Kell wakes with a groan and rolls onto his back.

I'm not in the States, he thinks. I'm near the equator, in an Asian land grown over with jungle. And I'm in love, he thinks, with a woman who's afraid of a giant snake.

He feels through the dimness to the head of the bed, then right to the bedpost and up it. The hibiscus mask is where he'd hung it. His fingers touch its chin, its smooth cheek, its empty eye orbit and the loop of tendril where the ear would have lobed.

Kell exhales, turns on the bedstand lamp and retrieves his phone.

When Yrine answers, he tells her about Nitti's "dazed" state, and he mentions the pills she takes. Yrine seems surprised.

"Has something like this happened before," Kell asks.

"I have no idea," Yrine replies.

"You knew her when you were children," he says.

"We started school together."

"You met her mother?" he asks.

"I did. Nitti's told you about her?"

"A little," Kell says.

"Do you know what a '*bomoh*' is?" Yrine says.

"Vaguely." A bomoh was a Malaysian who practiced sorcery in the days before reason and science.

"Some thought Ibu was one," Yrine says. "The woman was crazy. And cruel."

"Nitti talked to you about this?"

"When we were kids," Yrine says.

"She didn't believe the 'bomoh' nonsense."

Yrine hesitated. "I'm not sure."

The reservation in her voice made Kell shiver.

"She was very young," Yrine says.

Kell was thinking of Prawan, her influence in the house and her strange ideas.

"I've been asked to give Nitti some breathing room," he says, "but I'm worried about her. Can you make sure she's okay?"

A celebration is in progress at the Ginger House. In the open-air enclosure, three potted spindle gingers are elevated on a scarf-covered crate, and a lab tech is passing cups of juice around.

"May you beauties," Kell addresses the plants, "live long and fruitful lives."

He raises his cup, and the six members of his team join the toast. The PCR tests had verified that the wished-for edits occurred, and the three plants are thriving outdoors. But while the fete is a boost for his group, the memory of what had happened the previous week casts a shadow over

Kell. His attachment to Nitti included a wish for change, as if he could excise her fear as he would a sequence of code.

As the team returns to work, Kell looks up to see Susilo limping forward, his chin raised in greeting.

The visit's a surprise. Kell had heard some uncertain news from Yrine. He'd called Nitti multiple times, but there had been no response. Six days have passed since her strange eclipse.

He waves to Susilo, leaves the green wire cage and steps down the path to meet him. The old man's hug is firm, but his gait seems slower and his face is drawn. A black butterfly—a solemn Mormon—flits from a glade, passing over Susilo's shoulder.

"How is she?" Kell asks.

"Better," Susilo answers. But he sighs, as if there is much to explain.

Kell escorts him to the office and closes the door to the lab.

"I owe you an apology," Susilo says. "We both do. She was very confused that night."

"As long as Nitti's alright."

The old man looks weary. He'd been carrying a burden, it seems, and is ready to set it down. Kell clears the books from a chair, and the old man settles onto it.

"You and Nitti—" Susilo shakes his head. "The bond you found. It was all so unexpected." He lays his cane across his knees. "I wanted to believe it was for the best: the emergence of deeper feelings, the exploration that's part of romance. But—" He closes his eyes, as if what he's about to say will cause pain or regret. "I've been concerned. For her. What you saw a few days ago has happened before."

Kell is silent.

Susilo opens his eyes and looks at him. "She was unreachable."

"Before?"

"Once," the old man says. "Just once."

"When?"

"She was sixteen. They called it a 'break.' A 'catatonic break.'"

Kell hears the grief in his voice. "They?"

"The doctors," Susilo says. He touches his lapel. "It happened two weeks after my first heart trouble. I blamed Ibu for both."

He squints at Kell. "Her hatred had no limit. She expressed it freely to Nitti. Ibu dredged a dark fear in our daughter." The old man's gaze retreats. "My poor little girl."

The words are barely audible.

"Nitti was a beautiful flower," her father says. "She had a natural grace and charm. Ibu called her 'my pretty affliction.' She threw screaming fits at Nitti. One night before leaving for Keributan, she told our daughter she wished she'd never been born."

The beautiful flower, Kell thinks, was watered with poison.

"It all led to the 'accident.'" He removes a handkerchief from his chest pocket and wipes his mouth. "You've noticed the scarring around Nitti's eyes?"

Kell nods.

"That was self-inflicted. She was trying to disfigure herself."

Kell is speechless.

"You know about our rengas trees," the old man says.

Kell had seen what rengas could do to a man's arms—the eruptions and ulcerations.

"She put rengas sap on her face," Susilo says. "It swelled horribly, her eyes disappeared— She was in bed for weeks, feverish, lost in fearful delusions.

"She imagined Ibu was the snake in the swamp. At night, Nitti said, Ibu came to her room."

Susilo's eyes were drowned in sorrow. Kell shook his head.

"'I've seen her change,' Nitti said. She imagined Ibu's eyes turned orange. She saw the snake's reticulations on her mother's back. She saw Ibu's hips shrink and her legs fuse. Nitti was afraid to move or speak. The snake of Keributan, she said, would bind her, squeeze her breathless and swallow her whole."

Kell remembers Nitti's frozen face, her features blank, the ceiling fan turning above, its blades reflected in her sightless eyes.

"That's why she takes the pills," Kell says.

Susilo nods. "That's why."

"The 'break,'" Kell asks. "How long did it last?"

"It was seven months," the old man says, "before Nitti spoke. She spent that time at Tanjung Rambutan. You know the place?"

The limestone corridor of the Kinta Valley traps the heat at midday. With the windows down, Kell leaves the highway and takes the branch north. His overnight bag is on the floor below the passenger seat; and on the seat, facing up, is the hibiscus mask. At the last minute before leaving, he had taken it from the bedpost. His mind is full of Nitti, worried for her, longing for her. And the mask is his talisman now, his way of seeing the barrier between them and imagining how it might be cleared.

Tanjung Rambutan is a town and a district north of Ipoh. It's also the name of the oldest mental hospital in the country, located there. Kell had never been, but he knew about it like everyone else. Opened by the British during the colonial era, its first residents were opium addicts and victims of terminal syphilis.

The admittance booth comes into view, a glassed-in blockhouse with people in uniform inside and out. Kell waits in the car queue, speaks to a woman with epaulets, explaining his purpose. "No photos," she tells him, "stay in your vehicle." She waves him forward as the boom gate rises.

The road is well maintained and lined with palms, lawns extending on either side. A three-story building appears with signage. Unnamed structures, single story, then a cluster of duplexes ringed by gardens. A large cream-colored building appears on the left. "Main Hospital," the sign says. It has a covered car entrance and wings on either side. Counseling, he thinks, injections and surgery, shock treatment and psychedelics. Past the hospital is a paved lot with ambulances. Beyond that is a fourplex identified as "Admission Wards."

Kell imagines Nitti being checked in. A teenage girl, terrified and impenetrable, unable to speak.

On the right, a sign says "Rehabilitation." These are the bungalows where Susilo said Nitti had stayed. Set back from the road, with lawns that end at chain-link fences, they're like cottages from a children's fantasy. Lemon walls with apricot eaves and pink shutters. The windows have grills on them.

Kell fixes on one, imagining Nitti inside. She was watching the sun set through the bars, thinking of Ibu, the hungry python and the boundless sea of Keributan.

Just before she was released, Susilo said, he had tried to kill the snake. He bought a sick calf to use as bait and sat in the swamp with a firearm, waiting for it. But the python never appeared.

On the right, beyond the rehab cottages are larger buildings, and the fences around those are topped with barbed wire. Permanent residents, Kell guesses. They will stay there until they die. On the left are buildings signed "Forensics." He tried to imagine what it had been like, living among violent criminals and the incurably insane. Had Nitti mingled with them? A chilling thought, and bewildering too—that such alarming encounters might have occurred in this bucolic setting.

Beyond the dwellings, the grounds are park-like—grassy fields and rising hills planted with trees. Kell pulls aside, and with the engine idling he pictures Nitti walking there, mounting one rise after another, trying to free herself from the gulf she'd fallen into.

Keributan. Had she left it in Ipoh? Or had the ripples and swirls erupted here, without warning? Had she seen a boil rising like a bubble of gas, a surfacing head, an opening maw, and the jaws of the python closing over its victim?

On the drive back, Kell mulls what Susilo had said about the decision to commit his daughter. A family like his would seek help from the local mosque, treating an affliction like Nitti's through prayer. But Susilo was nervous about trusting holy verses or cleansing with limes. "And I wanted her away from Ibu." Nitti's stay at Tanjung Rambutan, combined with the years of Ibu's malign behavior, left the family estranged. Susilo still prayed at the mosque, but the community thought the family was cursed.

Kell now realized how wrong it would be to blame Nitti for the life she'd led. When she returned from the States, the ostracism would have made it impossible for her to be a Muslim wife. The paths that were open to other young women weren't open to her. Through the "arrangements," she had supported her father and the family home.

As Kell heads south, the weight of Nitti's hardships joins the fatigue he feels from the heat. When he enters Ipoh, melancholy overcomes him. He pulls his car to the curb and stares blindly through the windshield, remembering Susilo's words about Ibu's stroke. "With her mother silenced and out of sight, I hoped Nitti's fears would fade."

Kell opens the door, steps out, turns one way and another and starts down the street. Lorries, car horns, a motorbike tears past. A hobbling woman with a bindi catches his elbow, begging for change. Farther along, a younger one dances puppets for kids while a boy bangs a gong with a stick. Freeing your spirit, letting it speak— Who can do that, he thinks, but the vulnerable child?

Tubs of shrimp, fish heads and tails; a dim sum diner; a hardware store; then his stumble halts. Octagonal mirrors hang from the scissor gates of a framing store, and he's seeing his face in a silvered glass: a man fighting dread, a man with facts he's struggling to accept. Across the street, through crackling speakers, "You're Lost Little Girl" is playing in Chinese.

Fifty feet past the mirrors, a shop window is crowded with caskets. "Peace of Mind" the sign reads. Kell turns, crossing the street, stopping cars, headed for a derelict market, its bamboo blinds blackened with mold. The walls are cankered, paint clinging like scabs, scarred by wounds from a thousand monsoons. Before he'd left the Ginger House, Susilo confessed his uncertainty: he feared that the connection between them, something Kell had said or done, triggered Nitti's relapse; that her desire for him exposed her to danger. At the same time, Susilo said, he believed that love was what Nitti needed.

How could anyone know?

A break in the masonry, a narrow passage to a bricked courtyard. At the courtyard's rear, Kell sees a small building of darkened wood with a gondola roof, its eaves strung with red lanterns. Before the building's entrance, curtains are parted.

He passes a carving of an empty ark, a ship waiting for passengers. On his left, by the entrance, a Chinese couple sits at a card table. The woman smiles, the man motions him forward. The sanctuary interior is smoky and red, lit by a hundred candles. The floor is covered with polished tiles, and from it a dozen gold altars rise, carved and topped by counters of red enamel.

Here, red means health and longevity. But the well-wishing doesn't touch him. What reaches Kell is the smoke.

On every altar there's a large incense pot, each with a score of sticks burning; and the esses of fragrant smoke are a presence watching over a better world. Here, things are serene. In this untroubled place, truths could be thought and feelings felt, as in the Secret Chamber of Nitti's youth.

Beneath a lapping of nested proscenia, elaborately carved, lies the heart of the sanctuary, and as Kell steps into it the carvings come alive: serpentine forms, alarming creatures, dragons with wings, lizards and snakes—

But no. When you look more closely, there's nothing to threaten, no reason for dread. Only puddled clouds, winding mist and curling fog. Dreamy phantasms.

Has he wandered into a mystical incitement, a hint of paradise? Or is the combed flow, the whispering rhythm, the heavenly scent just smoke from an opium pipe. Seductive and dangerous.

Had he asked for too much from Nitti? What he wanted— Could she give it to him without imperiling herself? They were no longer children, either of them. The time when hearts were pure was past. Below the live sticks, weeks of burnt fragments were piled like ghostly pasta, the color of ash.

Kell steps out of the sanctuary and crosses the courtyard. The sun has passed its meridian and is starting down the sky. It will be one of those magical twilights, he thinks, when everything glows and the world of solid objects becomes—for glorious minutes—liquid and bronze. Then the show will end and the night will come.

5

Kell turns the wheel, pulling onto the apron before Nitti's home. When the motor is off, he opens his overnight bag, puts the hibiscus mask inside it and leaves his vehicle. Making a point of respecting Kell's arrival, Susilo motions him toward the right stair and greets him at the top. Then, supporting himself with his cane, the old man escorts Kell onto the veranda.

Nitti stands by the rail, facing the river, dressed in a gold lace top and a cream sarong. Her hair has been braided in a meticulous crown, and a scarlet hibiscus is pinned to the back of her head. She turns at his approach, mature and composed, the same Nitti he'd met at the Qing Club.

She sighs and reaches for his hand. "I don't know why—"

"Why what?"

"Why I was so frightened."

She's referring to her mental break. Trying to act calm,

but she's nervous. There is no hiding that.

"I'm glad you've come," Nitti says.

She was like an actress emerging from behind stage scenery.

"Sorry I'm late," Kell says. "I was at Tanjung Rambutan."

Susilo, who'd been watching them, bows his head and retreats.

"I drove through the place," Kell says. Then gently, "I wish you had told me."

Her rigor fades. A childlike smile appears—a tentative, helpless smile. Kell can see and feel the mask she's wearing, and the way it changes when the adult gives way to the little girl. Where had it come from? he wonders. When had she put it on? Maybe she'd returned from the hospital with it.

"You were glad to come home," he says, watching for her reaction.

Nitti looks down, picks at her nails, awash in misgivings. She straightens and gazes across the veranda to the waterside wing. "Ayah did what he could to keep her away from me." Her eyes are dark.

The waters of Keributan, Kell thinks, aren't pooled in the swamp or swirling beneath the boards of Ibu's room. They're clapping and circling inside Nitti.

"That didn't work," she says. "So he sent me to Boston. Boarding school and college. I found the job I told you about. Father hoped I would remain in your country."

"But you came back."

She sighs. "Ibu had her stroke. I thought the ordeal had ended."

"And?"

"When the testament was read, we learned that neither of us owned a thing. I couldn't abandon him."

"That was— How long ago?"

"Ten years," she says. "I was twenty-four."

There was irony in her eyes.

"I looked for Taseen," she says.

"Did you find him?"

She nods. "In Tapah. His wife was pregnant."

Nitti peers at him, measuring his acceptance. Then she links her arm through his and leads him back across the veranda. "I missed you," she says. "More than you can imagine."

Ten years, Kell thinks. She'd lived in this house, bathed, tended her wardrobe, walked the river and entertained men.

They pass through the outside door and start down the corridor.

She's escorting him to her bedroom.

Was it loyalty to Susilo that had kept her here, he wonders. Did she really have no other choice? Or was it some dark conviction about her fate. Was she wedded to the fear she'd known as a child?

They reach her door. She twists the knob and they enter her room.

Nitti turns and asks him to unpin her hibiscus.

He removes the blossom. It's red and soft with a dusky cast, like erogenous tissue.

"Loosen my top," she says.

He sets the hibiscus aside and undoes the catch. She

removes the lace top, baring her poreless shoulders. Kell runs his palm down her back, so flawlessly smooth.

On the dresser there's a pull toy, a cricket on wheels. Another memento of Nitti's childhood.

"Untie my sarong."

Kell is motionless. "I've found a specialist in Singapore," he says softly.

"Untie me please."

He does as she asks. The fabric parts and her thigh appears.

"I could look at you from across the room and make you hard," she says.

Nitti is resolute and commanding. Her face is as stiff as a mask. She turns to her vanity, takes the drugstore jar from the drawer and shakes a capsule into her palm.

"Take one," she says.

"Why would I do that?"

Kell sees the glint in her eye.

"Things will be easier for you," she says. "You're with a crazy woman."

She places the capsule between her lips and swallows it.

"Well?" she says.

Kell looks at the jar and shakes his head.

Nitti puts the jar on the counter and points at the floor. "On your knees."

"You were going to stop wearing the mask with me."

"We're playing," she says, as if to remind him.

Kell lowers himself.

"Kiss my thigh," Nitti directs.

He stares at her face for a long moment, feeling its distance. Then he puts his lips to the flesh of her leg.

"You're dangerous to me," she whispers. "Don't forget that."

Nitti takes the hand mirror from her vanity and turns it toward him.

Kell watches himself draw her panties down.

Maybe it was Kell's new awareness of the threats Nitti faced, his new doubts about his ability to understand her. Maybe it was a weakness bred by science, his feeling of ignorance and the limits of reasoned induction. Whatever the cause, the result was concession, assent—a yielding to his own helplessness. If by instinct Nitti knew what she wanted, the best course might be to assume she was right. Her fears, her strange journey, the visions she'd drawn him into— His promise of faith to her, it seemed, bound him to be her companion in that.

He's lying on the cobbled shore of the boundless sea, the black waters rumbling and hissing close by. Keributan is like a human presence, sensing him, awake to his thoughts and feelings. Above him the lone tree looms, naked and bleached, with the giant python coiled on its projecting branch, looking down. Its skin glitters with secret patterns. Its orange eyes burn with hunger and the strictness of forced delay.

In his dream or somnolent fantasy, Kell rolls onto his shoulder.

A young woman, sixteen perhaps, is stretched on the cobbles beside him, resting on her hip, wearing the hibiscus mask. It's gold with green streaks, but its features are Nitti's. It's cracked and in pieces: a cheek, part of the nose, one eye orbit and a sweep of brow, all stitched together with leaves and creatures.

The bird flutters over her brow, the ear-loop lizard tail twitches; then her seed capsule eye turns in its hole, the cheek swells and the mouth's corner draws in, smiling to itself.

"Our wish," the mask whispers, "the wish of knowing another, sharing a mind and heart. You remember that?"

I remember, he thinks.

"Of course you do," she continues. "And we are no longer wishing. No longer expecting, no longer throwing red blooms at hope. We are together now. I am the one, the one you sought out, the one you adore."

There's life in the mask's detail, its private freedom, its exotic allure. Despite its disguising purpose, it is fragile and daringly balanced; and with all the dangers, it is still unafraid to declare its need.

"What I want for you," the mask says, "I want for myself. To accept who we are. Without qualification, without reservation, however hidden we must be, however occluded our vision, however glancing our touch, however muted our voices. I will shield you, Kell—and you must shield me—from things too deeply felt."

She is preaching the Gospel of Secrets.

"We're secure," Nitti says, "in our bed of love. Devoted.

Committed. Pledged to each other and immune to fear."

Could she not feel the cobbles, he thinks. Did she not see the snake in the tree and the vastness of Keributan? Kell raises himself. He's about to speak when Nitti lifts her arm and puts her finger to his lips, as if she is hearing his thoughts.

"What will it take," she says, "for you to protect me?"

The next morning, Kell wakes alone in Nitti's bed. He can hear the shower running. On the nightstand he sees another plaything from Nitti's youth: a tin girl riding a tin scooter.

He throws back the sheets and, naked, he leaves the bed. Kell retrieves his overnight bag from the floor beneath the vanity and sets it on the counter. He opens it, removes the mask, feeling its cheek with his thumb, wondering at the way it's become a cipher for Nitti's mysteries. Then he dismisses the thoughts, looks around the room, steps toward the dresser and opens the top drawer. As he slides the mask beneath his underwear, the door latch clicks. When he looks up, Prawan is shuffling toward him, fresh linens draped over her arm.

"It's time you got dressed," she grumbles.

Kell closes the drawer.

Prawan sets the linens on the vanity stool, grasps the counterpane with both hands and strips it away.

He turns to recover his clothes. Avoiding conflict with Prawan was like keeping a tree between yourself and a wild boar.

"You'll be wanting breakfast, I suppose." She's removing the sheets, bundling them up.

"I'm going to drive into town and get some dim sum."

"It's a foul job," she mutters, "scrubbing out what you leave on the bedding."

Kell drives to Old Town and returns forty minutes later with two bags of food.

Nitti is in the bedroom with Prawan. A fresh sheet covers the mattress, and Nitti is on it, lying on her back in a robe of blue silk. Two red hibiscus blooms cover her eyes, and her hair is bound up in a towel. Prawan stoops over her, using the fingers of both hands to spread white clay on Nitti's face.

"I'm here," Kell says. Nitti's toes flutter.

He sets the bags down, retrieves a bun and holds it to her lips. Nitti takes a bite.

When Kell offers to do the same for Prawan, she gives him a vexed look. She's wearing a canvas smock, running her thumbs past the tails of Nitti's eyes, smearing the white ooze under the eaves of her brow.

"Nitti's skin," Prawan says, "comes from her mother. There's not a fold or a wrinkle on the girl's body. But you know that, don't you." Then to Nitti, "It's a crime she's given it over to coarse hands."

"Mine, you mean," Kell says.

The housekeeper doesn't reply.

"Her face would be perfect too," Prawan says, "if she hadn't put poison on it."

Nitti stiffens.

"The scars are barely visible now," Prawan mutters. "I've erased most of them."

"Ibu didn't care for Nitti's appearance," Kell says.

"That's a lie," Prawan replies.

"Maybe it was back then," Kell says, "that Nitti fashioned a mask for herself. The one she wears day and night, even with me."

Nitti was silent. So was Prawan.

"When was it?" he asks. "Do you remember?"

"I've had to protect myself all my life," Nitti says stolidly.

"That's not true," Prawan scolds her.

"Hush," Nitti says. Then to Kell, "My earliest memories—I wanted to be invisible."

"You wear the mask with men," Kell says.

"I do." Nitti's voice is icy.

Prawan sighs. She's dabbing clay beneath Nitti's ears.

"I've worn it in bed with them," Nitti says, "and with the python as well, when it comes to me in the night and stretches beside me."

Nitti spoke as if she was oblivious to Prawan's discomfort.

"How could that help?" Kell asks her.

"I pretend the snake doesn't know me. It can't see me."

"Did you use the mask," he asks, "to protect yourself from Ibu?"

"Enough," Prawan says.

"I did, it's true," Nitti says. "I wanted to hide myself. I didn't want her to see me or know what I was feeling."

Prawan has reached her limit. "Ibu cherished you," she says. "She was so excited to be carrying. She ate a blue fly-catcher every morning to give you a beautiful voice. She ate crickets too, to strengthen your limbs, and lizards to make your mind sharp, which it certainly is."

"Be quiet," Nitti demands.

The housekeeper huffs in frustration. She opens the neck-line of Nitti's robe and begins to massage the flesh above Nitti's breasts, clenching and pushing with the heels of her palms, her hostility unconcealed.

Kell sees Nitti's lips twitch. The white clay on her face is cracking now, but still attached.

That evening, Kwik's meth-head nephew reappeared. He escorted a Chinese street girl through the dining room as Kell and Nitti were eating. The boy wore a sleeveless tee, num-bered and splashed with color. Beneath his buzzcut, his eyes shifted like a cartoon spy. Nitti traded a few words with him while the girl fussed with her purse. Then the nephew and the street girl continued toward Susilo's room.

Ten minutes later, in Nitti's bedroom, over the sound of her showering, Kell hears the drone of the rempit's motorbike crossing the apron, heading back to town.

Kell goes to the dresser, opens the top drawer and takes

the hibiscus mask from beneath his underwear. He is standing there, looking at it when Nitti emerges from the bathroom. She comes up beside him, wrapped in her towel.

"What is that?" she says.

"I came across it in a market in Georgetown," Kell says. "I think it's helped me understand what you went through as a child."

"I'm sorry," she says.

Kell sets the mask on the dresser and grasps her shoulders.

"You could find someone else," Nitti says.

"It's you I want," Kell tells her. "I'm in love. I care about you." He pulls her against him. "If it's protection you need, I'll protect you. Tell me how I can make you feel safe, and I'll follow your lead."

"When I have troubling thoughts," she says, "sometimes I'm able to stop them. But sometimes—"

"I understand," he assures her.

"Worries," she says, "that won't leave. Questions that keep me locked inside, searching for answers. Pictures, movies that won't stop playing; terrible things, Kell. Things no one can see."

"I'm here," he says. "Remember I'm here."

"You know me," Nitti tells him. "Wanting to hide—" She raises her hand and touches the carved face on the dresser. "This terrible mask— I need it Kell. I'm not right without it." Her voice strains, rising in pitch. "I don't want to go back there."

"You're not going back," he says.

Their embrace is tentative at first. Even with familiar endearments and actions, Nitti seems remote and withdrawn. Kell is cautious, letting her steer, allowing her to set the pace and determine the direction.

With the distance between them, there's no way to be sure— But as desire leads them into the late hours, Nitti seems to grow bolder. The things she suggests to him are increasingly unfamiliar. She's coaxing him along, and in this new alignment she seems to be finding some comfort.

The room is dim, lit by a flickering flame. The drapes are open, the window's ajar. A pause, a hiatus. Kell is drawing quick breaths, on his side.

A flying lizard crosses the pane, webbed ribs sprung from its sides. Beyond the house perimeter is a world of subtle, concealed things: a cryptic moth pressed to a bole, leaves rustling in a breeze, the cry of a scops owl on the wing. How much does Nitti see or hear? She's as unaware, he thinks, as a camouflaged toad, black lilies or a dead-leaf mantis— creatures who were born to hide themselves and do so without even knowing.

Nitti's naked beneath the sheets. He's naked on top of them, facing her now. He's about to draw back the bedding for her, but she does it herself. What is she thinking? He has adored every part of her body in the past, but the adorations have been on his own impulse and by his own invention. Tonight is different. He is to mute his interior voice. Nitti is speaking now, and his job is to listen.

She has something in mind, something she wants. She

looses a stagey sigh—from a parent perhaps, who pretended to be a great actress—and the line of her smile spreads, its tail turned up. Then her lips move, ruling the dimness, issuing directions.

Kell curls around, obeying, facing her knees. And as she continues to speak, he does as she says. The flesh of her calf is velvety, soft as the top of a polypore conk. He has poured his affection over these legs before, but never under orders. The distance stirs him, and so does his lack of authority.

She continues to speak and Kell responds, moving to her ankle and around it. The knob, the wonderful knob at her tibia's end; then her instep, familiar but never so exalted. Back and forth. Slowly, Kell, much more slowly— At her request, he pauses, playing the gecko, cleaning his eyes with his tongue.

He's listening carefully, and she's explaining. In the candle flicker, he can see her toes spreading above him in anticipation, like the moment a leafbird opens its wings. And in a heartbeat, he understands: Nitti knows what he will do, and how she will feel when he does it.

Slowly, with the care she requests, he moves his tongue up the instep's fleshy corridor. A hesitation between the two eminences of her sole, waiting for guidance. Her commands don't come quickly, but when they come, they're precise. This, Kell thinks, is how he's going to protect her. There will never be a moment when she's unexpecting or unprepared.

Her toe pads are like dischidia leaves—perfect pebbles, perfectly round, perfectly smooth. Each toe cushion has its turn, as Nitti has defined it. Each will be touched by his tongue in the order that she's determined—not large-to-small and not the reverse, but in a sequence devised by her and re-layed to him just before the devotion is due. The toes flex and bow, exposing their polished topsides, piquing his doubt. Is she pleased with him? It seems that she is, but to be sure, he asks. Nitti's features are shadowed, but a forefinger appears in front of her lips, raised to quiet him.

He feels her hand on his hip now, urging a change. Kell curls around, approaching her face with his own, hearing her breaths, feeling her wind like beating wings. Is it wood come alive or human flesh—a face or a mask? A waving frond hides her eye. The other has a trap-door lid with a spider behind it. A bird's sharp bill needles his lip; his tongue is caught by a rope of ants, and they're pulling it, pulling it. Then Nitti's lips part and new requests reach his ears.

In the jungle a creature is piping, another hoots, a third makes a scraping sound. He's rising among the leaves of climb-ers crowding two trunks, webbing the crowns; lost in vanilla orchids and staghorn ferns, twisting uncarias with grappling claws, binding bauhinias that steal the light and smother their hosts. The majestic crowns are just above, a horizon of leaves rounded and smooth.

Nitti is on her hands and knees. Beyond her ribs, he can see a single eye staring, watching him. Kell hears the warning call of langurs in the distance. Then a command emerges like a monstrous insect, a spiny jungle nymph, its thorax curled, a hidden creature pretending to be an artless plant.

It's not Nitti's thumping heart he hears—it's his own. And with every beat, another sound surfaces through the jungle's incessant speech. Signals, alarms, from this side and that, from below and a hundred feet in the air. Hordes and legions of wild creatures, every one of them somehow threatened, living in fear.

Nitti—

Is he pleasing her? He's lost touch with desire, both hers and his own.

She folds onto her hip, speaking his name, reaching her arms toward him. Kell stretches beside her.

Nitti's lips are stiff, and her body is moving strangely against him—her arms, her middle, her thighs and calves. She seems to have lost her center. Her parts are shifting in different directions, at different speeds, as if she has many minds or is imagining many possibilities.

And then, in a moment, the parts cohere, sliding over him, tightening and coiling around him like a snake seeking heat to warm its blood. Had she come so close to the python that she'd absorbed its nature? Perhaps, by dining on fear, she'd turned reptilian: cold, cold-blooded, cold-hearted, cold in her core.

Then Nitti sighs and her body softens. Her tension drains out of him, along with the fear he'd been sharing. Her embrace relaxes, and her humanity seems to leak back.

"Are you there?"

She is whispering through her mask.

Kell returns to Jelutong and his work at the Ginger House.

The team, normally upbeat, is grumpy and glum. So many things could go wrong, and in Kell's absence, so many have. An edited kaempferia is crippling every ant that crosses it. The new alpinias are emitting something airborne that withers the nearby plants. Changed costus blooms have attracted hornets, and a white hedychium is turning its soil black. Kell does his best to raise their spirits. The group accepts its failures, destroys the faulty plants and begins a range of fresh edits.

Nitti's call comes at the end of the week. She asks him to pack enough clothing for a longer stay. Kell notifies his staff and the Gardens' management, and leaves the next morning.

When he arrives, Susilo escorts him to Nitti's room. As Kell enters, he calls to her. She replies, and when he cracks the bathroom door, he sees her stooped over, shaving her leg.

Kell puts his overnight bag on the bed and opens it.

He places his toiletries on the vanity counter, hangs his shirts in the armoire and puts his pants and underthings in the top dresser drawer beside Nitti's bras. As he closes the drawer, his eye falls on the mask he'd left on the dresser. He picks it up and peers at the carved visage.

At home with fear, Kell thinks. Living with dread.

Through a part in the window curtain, he sees Kwik pruning a tree in the orchard. He opens the window and calls to him. "Hammer," he shouts, holding up his pinched finger and thumb and swinging his arm like he's driving a nail.

Two minutes later Kwik is beside him, knees on the mattress, putting a tack in the wall over Nitti's bed. Kell hangs the hibiscus mask on it.

The gardener pats his shoulder, flashes his toothless smile and departs.

Kell stares at the wooden face, the carved seed pod hanging in its empty orbit, lizard tail looped in the place of a lobe, frog toes raying from the corner of its mouth—

The sink tap turns off.

Nitti appears wearing only a shirt, patting her damp legs with a towel. She kisses him, then faces the mask.

"An emblem of my respect," he nods. "A reminder of my promise to keep you safe—to accept whatever you choose to show me, whatever you wish to disclose of yourself."

"I'm grateful," she says.

Over the days that follow, they spend their hours together on the veranda, on the path by the river, in the dense woodland; and in bed, bound to each other, her voice in his ear, her needs in his head, desire passing from her mind to his. He follows her guidance, serving her demand for control. He's acutely conscious that the space between them is growing. The more distance he gives her, the more comfort she feels.

At first she ignores the wooden face hanging over their heads. But as Kell's stay stretches out and a single week turns into two, she begins to draw it into her thoughts and language. "The mask is my independence," she says late one night. For Kell, it's a borderland beyond which Nitti still lives. In the mask itself, he thinks, a ghost is entombed; and the ghosts of plants and animals are frozen there too.

While her distance disturbs him, there is no denying its healthful effects. Nitti's fear has diminished to such a degree that she's stopped taking her pills. Prawan scolds her to resume the medication, but Nitti refuses. And it does seem to him that, outside of their intimacies, she has a new tranquility. She seems more cheerful, less prone to dark moments. But in bed, her demands are taking them to even stranger places.

Kell is seeing things he wouldn't otherwise see. When the candle is lit, the mask watches them on the bed. The carved eye bulges like a carpenter bee backing out of a boring, measuring his prostration and his commitment to serve. The nostrils flare and the wooden lips part, drawing his scent in, weighing the musk of his attachment and the savor of his devotion.

"You know what's happening," Nitti says, "don't you?"

But Kell isn't sure. The mask is hiding so much. Is she affected deeply, or barely engaged? Is she constraining herself or trying to let go? With the freedom from observation, in the space the mask gives her, have her emotions expanded? What is she feeling? With each passing night, she is more of a mystery.

While Kell feels his importance diminishing, the power of the mask is growing. It's pleased by his subservience and the gain in Nitti's confidence. But it's nervous about the strength and protraction of his shuddering moments. It prefers if Kell tames his conclusions. And then, to his surprise one night, it intervenes, stifling his completion, urging him to deny himself.

The mask wants him to be content with submission.

When exhaustion sets in, they sleep with their heads turned away from each other. Kell is no longer privy to the truth in her eyes or the subtle clues about what she is thinking.

He is alone with the mask and the jungle.

With his back to Nitti and the window open, Kell falls asleep with the sounds in his ears: the calls of macaques, the snuffling of frogs, the hissing of wind and the clatter of rain, the whir of winged seeds, spinning as they descend in showers.

How much time has passed? Is he going to let himself vanish into Nitti's world? Kell is still ninety minutes from Penang, still connected to his botanical mission, still thinking of the Ginger House and his work. He's making calls on his mobile phone, covering for delays, using time off and a feigned tropical illness.

At the same time, he's form-fitted to her, beside her all day and proving his devotion every evening.

It's long past midnight. The burning candle is down to a stub, and the flicker is dim. Kell is naked and half asleep. He rolls onto his hip, feeling the humid waft from the open window. A murmur of rain moves through the jungle.

Nitti isn't beside him.

Is she in the room? Has she gone wandering, like her wild mother? His speculation and the purling rain conjure an image: in a dismal ravine, vines and lianas are writhing like female forms, sighing and dripping, bending elastic legs, heads swooning, arching their backs and haloing their arms. Is Nitti with them?

No, Nitti is close—a few feet from the bed.

He can hear her breath. He can see her stooped over in the candlelit darkness.

She lifts her head. The hibiscus mask covers her face. Both of her arms are at her sides. How is the mask held in place?

Is there a breeze in the room? The carved leaves by her ear seem to turn, glossy side up. In the uncertain light the tendrils, the loops and windings, look alive. The top of her cheek seems to twitch. The mushroom cap covering one eye—did it shift?

Nitti moves, drawing closer to the bed. Why has she done this? What is her purpose? Does she mean to enforce some new isolation? Perhaps Nitti doesn't know what's happened. The mask is declaring its own dominion. The carved face has a life of its own.

Her thighs touch the mattress. Her head dips, and beneath her chin the scalloped grain is visible.

Nitti is sliding beside him. She speaks his name softly and puts her hand on his chest. He can smell her skin. Between the wooden lips, he can see the hill of her tongue, its papillae crossed by threads of spit.

Then a tendril cinches her lids together, and the light in her eye winks out.

Nitti? he thinks.

Her voice sounds in his ear—an order is given.

Without a word Kell obeys, raising his hand to touch her

neck. And at his touch, the delicate surface turns to wood. Carved, gold streaked with green. A wavy grain appears—

Kell feels weak. Without thinking, his hand falls, touching her breast, and where it lands, the soft flesh freezes. Her sleek middle, the corrugation of ribs— Her skin, her flesh is replaced by golden-hued contours with scallops and lines.

The curve of her thigh has hardened. And the edge of her foot, the knobs of her toes—

He's lying beside a statue of wood.

The richness of life—its hopes, its fears, its raptures and tribulations, its violent moods and emotions— The Nitti he knew is gone. All that remains is a motionless icon.

Kell remembers the carved acrobat he'd held in his hands.

Is this what you want? he thinks, asking the idol.

Nitti doesn't reply. How could she?

The rain mounts abruptly, moaning, rattling, battering the roof. Nitti hears nothing. She's wooden, silent, emotionless, absent feeling.

She's unreachable now.

Kell removes his hand from her, knowing she's disappeared from his life. There's no bringing her back.

Lightning flashes at the window, and the dream drags him down.

Kell wakes with the image of the wooden idol in his mind, and he wonders what he will find when he opens his eyes.

The Nitti stretched beside him, of course, is flesh and blood, alive and stirring.

Something is troubling her. Her brow is creased, her gaze averted.

Kell strokes her cheek. She sighs, then rises on her elbow.

He waits, but she seems disinclined to speak. Is she as downcast as he is? Is she lamenting the distance between them? They'd fixed on her safety. But instead of feeling closer, instead of reaching her center, instead of knowing the heart of Nitti the child, he'd become a stranger.

Fear had done this, he knew. Her fear. The role Nitti had given herself—the protected, commanding role—meant separation, loneliness for them both.

He clambers off the bed, steps to the window and opens it all the way.

Sounds of the jungle invade the room. The creak of rattans, bee-eater trills, droning hornets and ringing cicadas. There is danger in the wild, he thinks. Plants and creatures use every edge, every trick and deception, to harm each other. Biologists, too, underrated the threats. Some entered the jungle and never came out.

In a world like this, he thinks, the only relief is the narrow view. All the joy in life comes from myopia—things close to home, the things that answer our needs directly, thrilling work, passion for a mate, the fulfillment of family—miracles magnified through proximity. He had an instinct for that because he'd been safe as a child. Nitti had not.

He turns to the carving over the bed, seeing an untroubled

face, serene even—not a symbol of eclipse or an object of idolatry. It was a trifle a tourist might buy.

His pledge to make Nitti safe was foolish, Kell thinks. Burying fear was as bad as feeling it—maybe worse. He'd failed her. And he'd failed himself. They were losing each other.

Does Nitti know? Is she feeling the loss as acutely as he is?

She has her back to him. She's tying a wrap around her middle. She says a few words and leaves to help Prawan in the kitchen.

He dresses and exits the room.

The previous night, an atlas moth had gotten into the house. When Kell closes the bedroom door behind him, he sees it fluttering down the hall, batting against walls and windows. He halts before the door to the guest room.

He couldn't do that to her—depart without a word.

And he wants her. Desire is still inside him. But it's lonely desire, helpless need. The mask—the distance between them—has poisoned his heart.

Susilo limps toward him, head wobbling. Has the old man been drinking?

"You and I," Susilo halts, "deserve no pity or consideration." He raises his cane and touches Kell's shoulder with the ivory knob. "We should know better than to bury ourselves in the fleeting pleasures of a senseless world."

Then the old man catches himself and frowns. Through his ferment, he perceives Kell's doubts and the prospect of his retreat. And he guesses the cause.

"Sickness of mind," Susilo says, "is a curse some families carry."

Kell meets the doleful gaze.

"Did Ibu pass her darkness along?" the old man says. "I've worried about that for a long time."

They share their sorrows in silence, then Kell takes his leave, making his way through the guest room and down the left stair on his own.

He drives slowly, taking the route through New Town. The city of Ipoh, he knows, was named for a poisonous tree. Natives applied sap to the tips of their blow darts and used it to take squirrels and birds. The banks of the river were once crowded with ipohs, but the town fathers had felled them all.

The roadway turns at the river. As Kell drives beside it, he imagines he's paddling downstream in a dugout canoe. The sound of a wooden flute reaches him, and as the dugout rounds a bend, instead of a meander or tributary he sees Keributan rippling and vast, spanning the horizon. On a rise, a young Nitti has posted herself. He calls out to her, waving his arm. But she can't hear him. Her back is to him, and she's gazing as if in a trance at the black sea.

6

Kell didn't hear from her until the following evening, and there were only a few lines. "You didn't say goodbye," her text read. "Is everything alright?"

This is strange, he thought. Was she unaware of his isolation?

If she didn't know, she must have at least suspected.

He composed a few answers, but they all seemed too dramatic, too much an expression of despair and defeat. Despite feeling hopeless, he didn't want to give up. She was still in his heart. Or he wanted to believe she was.

In Jelutong, he felt a new solitude, waking and eating in the empty house—a place he'd rented with no thought of how long he would stay or who might join him there. He was eight thousand miles from home with no grip on life other than the one his research gave him, and his return to work did little to boost his spirits.

Questions had arisen about PCR tests for a number of explants, so Kell brought a case full of samples to USM to get detailed genotypes run. He delivered, as well, a batch of new gingerols for chemical analysis. While he was there, he received some unsolicited views on his projects from an uninformed colleague—a man who had embarked on a foolish quest. He was looking for symbiosis among parasitic plants and their hosts. Kell could see the underpinning of faith in the man's determination to find merit in destructive relationships, as if some master intelligence had worked out the design.

And in his irritation, Kell recognized his own cynicism. Like others disappointed in love, he saw naïveté wherever he looked. Rationalizing parasitic plants and changing ginger genomes was no different than wanting to know Nitti without her mask. The world had no interest in rearranging itself to meet man's desires. Life wasn't a lab. It was a jungle; and plants, women and men all belonged to it.

It's over, he told himself. It's really over.

Then an hour later, his hopes would rise. He had felt so strongly about Nitti. Even with the setbacks and discouragements, those feelings were still with him. Was he really going to stay in retreat and wait for the feelings to die? He should be fighting to keep the two of them together.

But the thought of her need for self-protection, her fears and her mental breaks, returned to smother his spirits. He had no experience with these kinds of things, and he felt a disabling incapacity in facing them. Who was he to judge Nitti's "mask"? Who was he to try to remove it?

On their fourth day apart, he gets a text from her. "I love you," it says. "I miss you. Please come back."

He thinks of many replies, but his mind is so unsettled, he can't decide on one. She was reading, in his silence, his dark state. Did she understand how her distance had hurt him, how despairing he felt? He was disappointed by their failing, and he was disappointed in himself. He wasn't the man he had wanted to be. He had given her a promise. He had asked her to trust him.

If they spoke by phone or in person, what would he tell her?

Two more days pass, and she sends another message. "Don't abandon me," it says. "I beg you, Kell. We'll find our way."

Her words touch him. Could they? She was a rare woman. Maybe they could, maybe they could. With her appeals prodding his gloomy heart, he takes an aimless walk through the Botanical Gardens. It's approaching midday and the sun is hot. The joey palms wave their diamond leaves; the limes sway, laden with fruit; the statuesque irvingia fountain their branches over him. He longs for the Nitti who revealed herself in the Secret Chamber, whose courage and need touched him so deeply. But the woman who wears the mask, who issues orders from behind it to protect herself—

His vacillation distresses him. Kell has never felt so uncertain, so changeable. Doesn't he know his own mind?

He stops before an aquilaria trunk with a gaping wound. The sap bleeding from it emits a blissful fragrance, like the incense burning in the octagonal guest room. And with that scent he feels a fresh welling of hope. The vulnerable Nitti— Her need, when she expresses it, is a wonder of nature. He could spend his life looking and never find another woman like her.

He texts her, and when she responds, he alerts his staff and heads for his car.

Optimism carries him to the bridge, but as he starts across it, troubling memories surface. The wooden idol, an object of worship, the coldness in Nitti's core— All at once, suspended above the furrowed waters, Kell knows his mind. He doesn't want it to end, but he can't lie. He has to be honest.

On the far side, he pulls over and texts her again, suggesting they meet for white coffee in Ipoh. This will trouble her, he knows. But the time has come. Nitti must decide.

When he arrives, it's past noon. He parks his car and enters the coffee shop, a cheery place brightened by skylights and windows. People are crowded around circular tables and the walls are hung with mirrors. Nitti is seated alone, and when she spots him she smiles. But the smile is forced. She can sense his state. She knows him too well.

She has ordered for both. There's a full cup before her and another for him. Kell sits. White coffee is an Ipoh tradition. Sweetened with condensed milk, it's creamy and frothy, the way a child would like it.

Nitti draws a breath and looks into his eyes.

"It's not over. Is it?" she says.

"I don't want it to be," he replies. "But," he gives her a helpless look, "I need someone who wants to be seen."

She's confused or pretending to be.

"Maybe it's not a mask," she says. "Maybe it's me."

Kell can sense her sorrow, but it's a private one.

"If it is," he says, "we'll never be husband and wife."

At that, whatever confidence Nitti has crumbles, along with her cheer. Her eyes search, the corners of her mouth fall; then her cheeks go slack and the confusion in her eyes is replaced with dread and a little girl's innocence.

"What have I done?" she says with a sob.

Kell doesn't reply.

"Please." She clasps his hand. "Not goodbye." Tears stripe her cheeks.

"What can we do?" he says softly.

She struggles to answer. "We'll leave. Start over in some other country."

"You're not serious."

She stares back at him. "I'll be—" She stops herself.

Kell sees shame and longing, but courage too. He squeezes her hand.

"I'll be brave," Nitti says, tears flowing freely.

These are the words he wants her to say. Can he count on them?

It's as if she's heard his thoughts. "I don't want to be safe," she insists, "I don't want to be in control. I'll trust you," she says.

It's the most vulnerable he has ever seen her.

"And I'll trust you," Kell replies.

The server appears and the shop comes back into focus. Faces are turned, all of them, listening, watching.

Kell pays the bill and they leave.

He follows Nitti home. Alone in his car, Kell remembers a woman he'd dated who was studying dusky langurs. Following troops in the wild, she'd discovered that infant monkeys were afraid of heights. They held on for dear life, crying as their mothers leaped through the crowns. They had to learn to overcome fear. And they did, with the help of those closest to them.

When they arrive at the house by the river, Susilo is waiting in the guest room. He greets Kell with a warm embrace, cane raised, patting his shoulder to welcome him back. "I'm glad you're here," the old man says. And then to Nitti in a warning tone, "Prawan's been in your room."

Nitti nods, turns and leads the way down the corridor. Kell follows.

When they enter her room, he sees a new reminder of childhood on the vanity counter: a wind-up monkey drummer. It's a menagerie now, a dozen playthings from Nitti's past. She's facing the bed. Two photos have been taped to the wall above the pillows and below the hibiscus mask. One shows a woman dressed in male clothing. In the other she's seated with an infant in her lap.

Kell looks at Nitti. "Maybe there's a message here."

She cocks her head, unsure what he means.

"Maybe it's time," he says, "to sweep Prawan and all this claptrap aside. You're not helpless. You're a woman now."

He can see the roots of fear in her eyes. But instead of accepting her fear and retreating, Kell raises his voice against it.

148

"Why won't the python leave?"

Nitti doesn't reply.

"Why can't you say goodbye to it?"

"Please."

"Why, Nitti."

She closes her eyes.

"Why?" Kell clasps her shoulders.

Her lips part as if something is choking her.

"Tell me," Kell insists.

Nitti stiffens and shudders. Then her shoulders sag and her head bows—as if, Kell thinks, some ruthless resistance has been overcome.

"Ibu is in my room," Nitti says. "Her hands, her body— She's naked and black. Covered with Keributan."

Kell imagines the crazy woman covered with sludge, standing beside her terrified daughter—Nitti lying in bed, late at night, trying to sleep or just awoken—this bed, the same bed on which he and Nitti had expressed their desire.

"I'm sorry," she says, "I'm sorry, sorry—"

Is she speaking to him or the memory of her sinister mother?

Kell holds her close, wanting her to feel his care. Too young to fight, he thinks. Too young to resist. The little girl had accepted the terror Ibu gave her.

"She's left the door open," Nitti says. "I can see it, moving over the floor. Its head is raised. Its eye is red. Its tongue is twitching, white at the tip, tasting the air. It's reached Ibu's leg. It's coiling beside her. 'It's hungry,' Ibu says."

149

There is no telling how much is real and how much imagined.

"It's looking at me," Nitti says. "It knows what I'm thinking. When Ibu touches it, the snake's skin twitches and the black patterns move."

"Maybe that's what she wanted," Kell says. "To put a fear in you that you'd never grow out of. To prevent you from being a woman."

"She can't do that," Nitti protested.

Was it really devotion to her father, Kell thinks, that has kept her here? If they left, would the fear follow her?

"You were with your mother," he says, "after her stroke?"

Nitti nods.

"Did you speak to her?"

She doesn't answer.

"What did you see?" Kell asks.

Nitti shivers.

"Tell me," he says.

Nitti's lips part. She tries to speak, but cannot. She swallows and tries again. "Her arm was bent. There was something wrong with her fingers. Two were crossed, the others were curled. 'She isn't able to straighten herself,' the doctor said. 'She can't move her head.'"

"So she's helpless," Kell says. "Powerless."

"Prawan says—"

His sigh of exasperation stops her.

"I'm sorry," he concedes. "What does Prawan say."

"Ibu's still with us—watching, thinking.

"After her stroke, when I went to her room—Prawan was with me. 'Talk to Ibu,' she said. 'Talk to your mother.' Prawan held my hand. We went down on our knees together. I could see Ibu's eyes. I was very frightened. I could barely speak. 'Go on,' Prawan said. So I tried.

"'I'm Nitti,' I said. Ibu didn't answer, so I moved closer. 'I'm Nitti, your daughter.' I've never been so afraid." She shakes her head. "But—"

"But what?"

"She couldn't see me. She didn't know I was there."

The latch clicks, the knob turns and the door opens.

Prawan stands there in her apron, regarding them both. "I've made lunch," she says.

Nitti ties her hair up and they leave the room, following the housekeeper into the dining area.

Kell and Nitti sit side by side at the table. On it there's a bowl of native herbs—pieces of scarlet hibiscus petal, peppers and sprouts, and the unopened leaves of a bird's nest fern. Another bowl holds four-angled goa beans.

As Kell reaches for the serving fork, Prawan puts her hands on her hips.

"I didn't think you'd come back," she says, regarding him critically. "Our interest in you is fading."

Nitti's lips part. She looks at Prawan, stunned and angry. "If Kell wants me," she says, "I'll be his wife."

Prawan's head bucks with a scornful laugh, jowls jouncing beneath. "You'll never get Ibu's approval."

"Stop," Nitti demands.

But Prawan isn't stopping. "It's time," she says, "to repay her. Your debts have come due." Her tone is irate.

Susilo is limping down the hall. He approaches the table, seeing the fare.

"*Ulam*," the old man smiles at the salad.

"Back to your room," Prawan orders him. "And don't come out."

Susilo's head turns as if he's been slapped.

Nitti's aghast. "That's enough," she says.

But Susilo is heading back down the hall.

Prawan glares at Nitti. "The hot food's coming," she says, and she turns on her heel and leaves the room.

Whatever forbearance the housekeeper had is gone, Kell thinks. She's an advancing army of termites now, clicking her pincers. If you got too close, she'd eat through your boots.

Nitti is serving salad from the bowl onto his plate.

Her words are echoing in his head. Despite all the obstacles, she wants to believe. And so does he.

"Would you?" he says. "Be my wife."

Nitti's eyes are grave. "I would."

"We couldn't be here," he says. "In this house."

"No," she agrees, "we couldn't."

"If I wanted to return to the States," he says, "would you come with me?"

"I can't leave my father," Nitti says.

"We could find a place—"

Kell stops himself. He hears Prawan returning, clapping up the stair from the kitchen. "Instead of laksa," she

152

announces to Nitti, "I made one of your mother's favorites."

Prawan steps toward the table, holding a glass baking dish in mitted hands. "We haven't had it," she says "in a great while."

With that, she sets the baking dish on a trivet.

The glass rectangle is crowded with monkey cups filled with steaming rice.

Kell had heard that *ampullaria* was sometimes prepared this way, but the sight is still a shock, considering the poisonous secretions and dissolved body parts the green urns had held.

"How dare you." Nitti is staring at the cups with eyes as black as Keributan.

She scoots back her chair and stands.

Kell rises with her. What had possessed Prawan, he wonders. Did she collect the cups from the peat swamp herself?

"You don't care a thing about me," Nitti says.

Prawan's lip quivers. She shrugs out of her apron and drapes it over one of the chairs, as if she's resigning her position.

Nitti glances at Kell and motions him away from the table.

Prawan faces him, looking miserably aggrieved. "You want to do some good here?" she says. "Persuade Nitti to soften her heart. The poor woman never sees her only child."

Nitti's heading back to her room. Kell follows.

As they enter, he catches her hand with his own. Her arm is quivering, her breath racing. "She's out of her mind," he says.

Nitti's too upset to speak.

"You shouldn't stay here another day." Kell turns her head

toward him. "We'll move you into my place in Jelutong until we can make other plans."

"My father—"

"We'll figure that out," he assures her.

Kell can see his words are registering.

"You're right," she says softly. "I don't belong here."

"There's something that matters," he says. "Really matters."

It's time to make his qualification explicit.

"We're done with this, aren't we," he says, eyeing the hibiscus mask.

"We are," Nitti replies. "No more hiding. No more secrets."

"I want the real you," Kell says.

"I'll be brave," she tells him. "I'm not afraid."

They talk at length, and in the late afternoon they leave the house, taking the slat bridge across the river. As they roam through the woods, they discuss Nitti's departure from the family home and what it will mean to uproot Susilo. He had accepted his circumstance and was expecting to live out his days there. They agree: Nitti and her father will pack the next day, and they'll move into Kell's house in Jelutong the day after that. From there, with the monsoon's approach, they will plot their escape from Malaysia.

Kell's research is far from completion. There are many more tests to run on the gingerols he's extracted. But he can see the end of his field work, he says—the end of his residency at the Botanical Gardens and USM. In a month or two, he'll be ready to return to the States. Nitti, from her time in Boston, knows what to expect. Immigration is a problem marriage will solve. She'll find a place for her father and help him with the adjustment. In the end, she hopes, he'll be better off.

Above them, there's wind in the crowns, leaves meshing and unmeshing, arranging a bright mosaic of sky. An arch-duke butterfly beats strong wings, gliding chest-high between a pair of sterculia trees. An opilion stick-walks over Kell's boot. On a stub of rattan, a white-throated kingfisher is scouting for frogs. In a thicket of climbing bamboo, a thin green vine snake makes delicate loops.

They stop beneath a russet paperbark tree. As Kell puts his arms around Nitti, a birdwave flies past—spiderhunters, leafbirds, two fantails and a myna—foraging together for safety.

Nitti kisses him softly, tenderly. "You're my Temple," she says.

"And you're mine." Kell holds her close, seeing their future together.

Then, as so often happens in the jungle, the sky rumbles and rain pours down, splattering the leaves, rilling in the bark furrows, soaking them both, driving them back the way they'd come.

That night in her room, Kell feels a new tranquility with Nitti, a new confidence in the future.

"Let's clean each other," she says.

She unbuttons his shirt. She loosens his belt and slides his pants down. "Now you undress me," she says.

Kell does that and when he presses her close, a fresh honesty seems to transfuse them. In his arms, he can feel Nitti's frame relax; and he tells his own body to do the same. They step into the bathroom together. Nitti turns on the tap, and when the spray is warm and the stall steamy, she leads him into it.

Kell feels a muzzy elation in the heat and vapor. Nitti soaps them both, and instead of rinsing, they just stand and sway together, feeling pliable, tilting, bending, sliding together.

The mask is gone, or so thin that it might be as easily removed as Prawan's white clay. With a sponge, Kell thinks, it would just scrub away. Nitti's eyes see and know; her mind is focused on a shared understanding; and her heart is yearning, starting to whisper.

She turns off the taps. He's holding her tightly. He kisses the crown of her head.

They towel themselves dry, return to the darkened bedroom and crawl onto the mattress together.

There's no candle burning. Through the window, the sky is black. The moon's invisible, and clouds have snuffed out the stars. But as Kell embraces Nitti, feeling her warmth, so close, so ready, he imagines the jungle is lit at every angle. Fungus on fallen trees glimmers blue-green, vines bristle with

156

fire, the soil is powdered with glowing sugar and crawling with luminous creatures. Trap-door spiders and golden cats, metallic green scarabs and rhino beetles, jet black with flashing horns.

He puts his lips to hers, opening his care and affection to her; and as his desire begins to declare itself, he can hear her heart speaking—softly, tentatively—trying to reach him. Trying to rise above halting gasps and the whispers of fear, wanting so badly to be recognized—

Louder, he thinks. Nitti, throw caution away. Earnest woman, brave child— Trust me and the chance that our fates are connected. I won't hurt you, I swear.

A whimper, a caught breath. Kell holds her close, feeling raw emotion streaming out of her, meeting it with a reassuring embrace, full and close and tight— Too much. He opens his arms and draws back.

She reads his retreat, and she's thankful. Now she's trying again, kissing his neck, the sound of surrender in her throat, mustering the courage to make herself known. Kell feels her inmost self advancing—rising, pausing. And shrinking back.

Her fingers freeze, nails hooked in the skin below his shoulders. Warning him, warding him off.

Why? he thinks.

And then, What should I do? Add more of his fuel to the sputtering fire?

Her hands open. They're caressing his back. She's kissing his cheek, opening her thighs, trying again— But stiffly, forcing herself.

I'm losing her, Kell thinks. She's frightened, divorced from her feelings.

Her hands slide from him. Her arms fall beside her.

"Nitti," he whispers. "We're in the Secret Chamber."

She hears his dismay, and it drives her heart still farther from him, into the swampy depths.

Nitti pulls away, rolling onto her side, shivering and alone.

Is the mask so much a part of her that it can never be removed? This, Kell thinks, is the true Keributan.

And it's as if he has spoken the words out loud. Nitti feels his doubt, and that opens the wound she received from Ibu when she was a child.

How can he help her? Or can he? Without the shelter of maternal care, life has been a jungle for her: vicious, perilous, full of deceptions and waiting atrocities. And despite everything, his desire for her is counted among them.

Rain beats on the roof. As if cued by their state, a storm descends on the sorry home. In the swamp, Kell thinks, rain is stirring the pools. The monkey cups are collecting fluid, fattening the soup of dissolved bodies—ants, termites, flies still twitching their wings. And the giant python coiled on the bough of the naked tree is lifting its head, thinking the time has arrived.

Nitti's face is invisible, hair spilled over it.

The hibiscus mask hangs on the wall, watching them both.

Slowly, Nitti raises her shoulders. As she turns her head, it's as if the mask's duplicate is rotating below it. But the mask Nitti wears is cracked. Some act of growth or anger has stressed it, dividing it into pieces. And between the shards, there is leakage—upset, aversion, contempt—a guarding presence with no feeling for Kell, no feeling at all.

A Prawan lives inside Nitti, he thinks, vicious, bitter and cold, guarding the sad little girl. And the deeper Nitti, soft and vulnerable— Where is she?

The mask's jaw moves: grinding discontent long suppressed. Fluid drips from the eyehole: distress verging on tears, rage or grief, without an evident source. As the pieces of the broken mask shift, Kell sees weaver ant silk, spiderwebs and white mycelia stretching between them, like energy flowing into and out of the wood.

And then strangely—beautifully—her deepest nature appears.

Shedding her fear, shrugging off sorrow, Nitti's eye meets his. Through the fragments of the breaking mask, Kell can see the brave woman beneath.

His future, he thinks. His hope, his belief— And his wife.

A muted scream. Did the wooden lips move?

No, a louder scream and shouting too, from somewhere else in the house.

Someone is calling for help, pounding on a door or a wall.

Nitti's head turns. She crawls to the mattress edge and stands. Another call and more pounding. Kell leaves the bed. Nitti throws a robe over her shoulders and whirls for the door. He pulls on his pants and follows. The noises lead them along the corridor, through the dining room and into the hall.

As they round the corner, a young Asian woman appears by the door of Susilo's room. She's naked, hair draggled, and a fading cry wheezes from her throat. When she sees them hurrying forward, her pounding ceases. Her fist falls and she begins to sob.

Prawan shouts and Kwik appears, scuttling behind her.

Nitti enters the room and Kell follows. Susilo is on the floor beside the bed, convulsing.

"Call for help," Nitti barks.

Kell finds the phone in his pocket and dials 999. Susilo's legs are rigid, but his chest is bucking. His neck seems twice its length, and at its end the bug-eyed head is wrenching, emitting agonized gasps.

An operator answers. As Kell makes the emergency request, he crouches beside Nitti. "Ayah, Ayah," she gasps. She has her arms around her father's quaking trunk, her jaw crooked with shock, tears streaming down her face.

"Let him breathe," Prawan orders and sinks to her knees between them. "You old fool," she mutters. "Look what you've done."

Kwik has hurried past them into the bathroom. He returns now with a damp towel and kneels, holding it to Susilo's quivering brow.

"Nitti," Kell whispers.

Susilo, amid his agony, sees the horror in his daughter's face and tries to open his arms. She buries herself between them, murmuring things Kell can't hear.

A few minutes later, the ambulance arrives. The medics

are able to calm Susilo's quakes. Then he's loaded into the emergency van and they depart with siren blaring.

Nitti collapses in Kell's arms, sobbing, venting her grief, dreading the hospital and the peril that threatens her father.

The young Asian woman, in a black dress now with a pearl purse over her shoulder, hair still amiss, leaves with Kwik for the guest room to await the meth-head nephew and his motorbike.

Kell escorts Nitti out of Susilo's room.

"He's not going to die," she says.

It's the battered, frightened child he hears.

As they pass the corridor to the waterside wing, Kell spots a large centipede on the pavers. Somehow they found their way into homes. A rusty body, a foot long, would wriggle across a rug or curl by an entrance as this one had. Like a sentry, posted and waiting.

7

ate didn't respect Nitti's needs or wishes. In the hospital, her father's decline was rapid, and he expired late that same night.

Prawan contacted a local imam, and with his guidance, she and Kwik accomplished the preliminaries. Susilo's body was washed and placed on the dining room table. With the help of Kwik's nephew and a couple of his rempit friends, the body was wrapped in white sheets and bound with packing cord. A casket was purchased, and arrangements for the burial were made. Kell did his part and covered the expenses. Nitti was unable to assist with practical matters, large or small.

From the hour of Susilo's death, her sobbing was constant. The quality of her tears changed with her emotions moment by moment—ardent heaves for remembered affection, piteous entreaties for his return, a brittle whimpering at thoughts of a future without him. It was as if, Kell thought, mourning her father's departure might protect her from the consequences of life without him.

He did what he could to help her, but there were times when he was unsure if she felt his presence or was comforted by it. He wondered where the sorrow would leave them when it reached its end.

With the prescribed three days of mourning behind them, the bereaved gather on the burial ground, downhill of an open grave, men in front except for Kell, who violates tradition and stands with Nitti.

She wears black with a matching head scarf. Prawan and Kwik wear white.

The wrapped body is laced with hibiscus blooms. The imam stands facing it, reciting prayers in a quiet voice. Nitti cries. Prawan mumbles along. There are tears on Kwik's cheeks, and from an adjacent lot, clutches of motorbikes rev together as the meth-head nephew's pals join the lament.

Kell circles Nitti with his arm as the imam turns his head and motions.

There are three men on either side of the casket, the buzz-cut nephew and one of his friends among them. At the direction of the imam, they grab the ropes and lift the casket. But before the box begins to descend, an explosion goes off; or rather a string of explosions, a sizzling and popping around the casket like a machine gun round. Smoke rises, along with flying bits of red paper. Someone had woven firecrackers into the casket's blooms. The meth-head nephew is giggling and shaking his shoulders, while the rev of motorbikes swells and a cheer goes up from a nearby plot. Kwik raises his arms to his nephew and laughs through his tears.

The imam scowls, but he's standing patiently, waiting for the red snow to fall and the clamor to fade. Then he signals again, the men lift the casket on its ropes and begin to lower it down.

Nitti has missed the moment of humor. Her hands are knotted by her throat and she's fixed on the burial pit, watching the casket descend with a horrified expression.

"What is it?" Kell whispers.

"Keributan," she murmurs.

The excavated earth is black. Rain that morning had turned the pit's edge to mud. As the box descends, slumps come loose. But Nitti is seeing something far worse. Her mouth gapes, her eyes grow wider.

She imagines her father is sinking into Ibu's black doom. The stroke victim has left the waterside wing, Kell thinks. She's here in the graveyard; and from the pit, she's conjured a bottomless well, narrow and cold and all-consuming.

The casket drops out of view, and as it does, Nitti trembles and her eyes seek his.

Kell can see the wounded child longing for her father's reassurance. He presses her close, trying to calm her, whispering that the appearance of the dark well is an unlucky illusion.

The casket reaches the pit's bottom, and a thud rises from the hole.

Kell is hiding Nitti's face in his shoulder. Then, feeling the depth of her disquiet, he turns her and leads her away from the gravesite. As they pass a knoll, her tears return.

"Ayah," she sobs. "*Jangan risau*—" It's hard to make sense of her words, as half are Malay and they're coming quickly. Then they slow and enough English creeps in that he understands. She's speaking to Susilo, reassuring him. He's beyond his ordeal now. And she's older, no longer helpless. She can defend herself.

In the car, as Kell starts back, her muttered grief continues. Slowly she seems to collect herself, and as they reenter the city, her tears stop.

"I don't want to go home," Nitti says.

Kell sees the plea in her eyes.

"Would you like to get something to eat?" he asks.

The river runs through the center of Ipoh, dividing Old Town and New. He steers into the right lane, thinking to turn onto a side street.

Nitti watches the grassy littoral pass. Without warning, she stiffens and points. "Here, stop here."

Kell slows the car and pulls to the curb. Nitti opens her door and motions him out.

As they step toward a concrete path that follows the river, he puts his hand in his pants pocket. There's something unexpected in it. He draws out the object—a miniature shovel, five inches long.

Kell's mystified for a moment. Then he realizes—it's from Nitti's childhood. The shovel is a message to him from Prawan: Nitti's first allegiance is to her mother.

She's gazing at the river. As he returns the shovel to his

pocket, Nitti links her arm through his and they start along the walkway. The waterfront is tree-lined, with people strolling and cycling. Men and women, couples old and young—a place for lovers and friends. Some were bound for life, Kell thinks, and some only wished. Some could open their hearts and some could not.

A suspension bridge appears ahead, a pedestrian overpass spanning the river.

"Have you been here?" she asks.

Kell shakes his head.

"It's 'Love Bridge.'" She sighs, feeling sorrow but hugging his arm.

Kell can see: ranks of locks, a multitude of them hanging from chains secured to the bridge railing. He knows of the practice. Other cities had similar bridges and similar customs; but for them, at this particular moment, the symbol might be important.

She's guiding him toward a shop in the lee of a riverside grove. In the midst of her grief, love isn't forgotten.

Inside the shop, scores of locks are arrayed on shelves.

"We could pick one," he says.

Nitti raises a heart-shaped lock with a skeleton key. On the silver face are twin circles, where the couple ink their initials.

"I like it," he nods.

When he's paid for the lock and they've made their inscriptions, they leave the shop, cross the pathway and mount the steel steps of the bridge. Halfway across, Nitti finds a spot, and they hang the lock on the chain with a thousand others.

Kell closes the latch with a snap. She holds the key over the railing and drops it into the water.

Nitti faces him and closes her eyes.

Kell kisses her.

"Do you think I'll be a good wife?" she whispers.

Then she laughs, removing the need to reply.

When they arrive at the house, Prawan and Kwik haven't yet returned.

Kell escorts Nitti to her room, seats her on the mattress and removes her black scarf and shawl. When he's returned them to her dresser, he steps to the vanity counter, opens the drawer and removes the pharmacy jar.

"For calm," he says. He pours a glass of water, spills a pill into his palm, and hands the glass and the pill to her. Nitti takes her medicine.

Kell, feeling her agitation keenly, spills out another, puts it on his tongue and swallows it dry. "Shall we rest awhile?" He seats himself beside her and unlaces her shoe.

"Ayah," she murmurs.

With all his flaws, Nitti had depended on her father.

He helps her to stand, and he unfastens her black dress. Then he removes his own clothing and they lie down together.

He holds her loosely in a gentle embrace. The window is open, and through it comes the fragrance of wilting cananga, the piping of a plaintive cuckoo and the thrum of the river, soothing and ceaseless. He caresses Nitti's back. Her finger curls over his chin. In the jungle, he thinks, the ceiling of leaves is glittering, leaded and paned with emerald glass; on the ground, light is pooling on fallen leaves and branches.

Then, abruptly, he's waking from sleep.

Time has passed, but in the haze from Nitti's pill, he's unsure how much.

The room is dark. Evening now. They'd slept through the day.

She's unconscious, he thinks. Then he feels her fingers beneath his thigh—invisible but sensing him, like leeches on the underside of a leaf.

She surprises him, her silhouette rising as if she'd been waiting for him to wake.

He feels her hand moving over his hip, into his groin, touching him in an unsubtle way. Hoping sex will separate her from her loss, Kell thinks.

"You know what I'm feeling," she whispers.

He wasn't sure he did, but he accepted her words as an expression of their connection and her hope for a future together. She wanted his love. She was going to survive her father's death.

"I trust you," she says. "No more hiding."

Her words enter his chest, seeking affirmation, searching inside him, ready to bare herself and find shelter with his own deeper self. She's returning, Kell thinks, to the precarious moment when Susilo's heart failed.

"I'm here," he whispers, priming her trust, believing in

them, in the bliss they might find if their natures were free to mingle.

Her face appears directly before him, emerging from the darkness as if in response to a vow or promise. One eye has a sealed lid; the locks by her ear are curled like tendrils; her wooden lips are frozen in a half-smile. Carved for him and everyone else. All defense and calculation.

Is he awake or asleep? he wonders. Asleep and dreaming, lost in a spell that the mask has woven—

Then before his eyes, a crack crosses the face from chin to brow, jagged as lightning. Through the crack, Kell can see Nitti's lips move, trying to express something long withheld. The closed lid swells, her hidden eye struggles to see him.

He has earned her trust, Kell thinks. And now it's happening.

She is opening herself to him, expecting him to do the same.

For the first time he wonders if he can abide with her in perfect vulnerability. She's aspiring to be the woman he wants, the woman he's always wanted. And then, as if in response, the planes of the cracked mask move, the closed lid bursts and a seeking eye peers at him. Her need is making its declaration.

The shape she'd been given long ago by someone else— It no longer matters.

Kell is facing the eye, seeing her naked innocence—not quailing, not turning away; but brave, confidence welling, losing stiffness and age—a teen, a grown child, or younger,

younger. Both of them, a girl and a boy. And in that enlarging moment, Kell sees something he'd never expected to see in Nitti or anyone else.

A slight curve in her upper lip. The faintest smile, absent humor or cheer; half a smile, or a quarter perhaps, lifted by peace and tenderness, and the warmest and largest affection this world knows. The feeling and then the recognition: in Nitti's lips he remembers his mother's smile.

Genuine love, the most precious kind: love that can only be found in an unguarded heart. Kell returns the smile, faintly, with gladness and an artless admission of need, feeling union, union at last, the long-sought moment of timeless tranquility.

He draws closer to the gap in the mask, to touch his lips to hers. The carved pieces shift like pads of water gentian floating aside. The shell of her ear cracks loose and sags. Her brow is an island moving free of her nose, carrying the wooden bird with it.

And beneath? Kell readies himself to see a Nitti he's never seen. The woman he thought he loved— Who is she really?

A diagonal chink, her chin comes free. In the spaces between the shifting fragments, he sees fibrous links stretching—spider silk and fungus hair. The jaw is loose, and there's a ticking and twitching beneath, like the sound of ants leaving their nest.

The hidden creature— Is it a finished woman or something else? He can only see lips and the top of her cheek. The pieces are loosening, but—

For a moment, Kell wonders if Nitti is just an impression without substance or depth. He can see the wildness beneath the pieces, the tendrils and vines, leaves and thorns, a snail's slime and a fantail's feather.

"Kell," the lips whisper, "don't leave me."

He can't, he thinks.

"I beg you," she says.

Whatever his role, Kell thinks: lover, confidant, defender, spouse— If the face of command vanishes for good— If the child never emerges from its shelter— Even if the pieces of Nitti he knows no longer cohere—

"You're all I have," the lips say.

"I promise," he vows, answering her need.

But a greater confusion is being exposed. Beetles and wasps are carrying parts of her face away. As the rigid flesh tears and the stringy mycelia snap, a chaos of worms and bugs appears in the gaps—

Nitti's still hidden. Can she feel his devotion? How far beneath the unpuzzling is she? Crushed by passion and yearning, Kell's mind lets go of its mooring, and the terrors that hold the mask together fully relax.

Grubs wriggle from a temple crack, and a bagworm bursts behind Nitti's nose. From her mouth, a flood of lacewings; from an ear, stingless bees; a leaf curled by a tailorbird lifts, and the nostril beneath is a cetonid's back. From a mat of fungus beneath Nitti's jaw, termites emerge; mycelial shreds stretch, attachments popping— The mask is a broken thing, but its pieces are seething with life: leafhoppers, wasps, harlequin bugs with needle noses, hollow-stemmed creepers like severed veins with streams of red ants flowing out—

In the interstices, hints of fresh flesh. Kell sees a brow gently eaved, a young woman's lips, the modest nose of a girl born to some tribe camped beside a river.

Rain. Rain is falling. Beyond his vision, beyond the mask and the creature beneath it, a black rain is falling through a black sky. Kell hears it at a distance: crossing ridges, stippling streams, slapping fan palms and wild bananas. And behind her dissolving mask, Nitti hears it too. She knows rain, the pounding monsoon, the indomitable flow of water and time, and the threats of the jungle.

Closer and closer—rain from an inexhaustible source. It's around them now, drubbing the hills, soaking the slopes. But it isn't a storm. It's a rain of ruined creatures, poisoned, dissolved—a black syrup from giant urns. Like clouds in the heavens, enormous monkey cups are turning over.

The nostril beneath the broken mask twitches, smelling Keributan.

Swamp mud, black ichor—

A drop falls on Nitti's bare chin, another dots the side of her brow. The fragments of mask are freckling black, the ragged neckline edging with ooze. Has Ibu's curse chosen now to descend, or has Nitti's desire for him given the poison its chance?

Kell hears a crying sound. A girl's despair—

Two old photos, a vase of scarlet hibiscus, the ivory knob of a dead man's cane—

Adrift, Kell thought, in a foreign land, dreaming that love was locked in a lemon box with apricot eaves and pink shutters. And now: he's in a dangerous place. The rain is pounding, the air striated, the black storm is moving the mass of the jungle as one. On either side, hillocks and banks are sloughing and sliding, losing their shape.

This rain, Kell knows, is a destroyer. It takes homes and people with it—their thoughts, their bodies, their flimsy identities—

Nitti is still before him, but standing now. Kell raises his hand, thinking he might resecure the fragments of mask. But it's too late. The pieces of wood are unpuzzled, detached. And as he watches, the last rotten fragments fall away.

The creature revealed is one he has never seen: an innocent girl, entirely unsuspecting, with a flawless and simple face; a girl unaware of threats portending, one who has no thought of shelter, of a Temple, of a boy named Taseen or a man named Kell.

The child Nitti is standing on a cobbled strand, confused and alone, while the black rain falls. Before her is the great sea of Keributan, and its waves are building.

All at once, the rain stops—abruptly, as if a switch turned it off.

Is it Kell's presence that's done this? No, he thinks, it's the vulnerable child. The black sea has no use for rain. It's no mere collection of drops and streams. Keributan is alive; it has a mind of its own, a proud and willful mind; and it does what it pleases.

Its currents are thickly threaded, firm as muscle, with a myriad ridges shifting across it. Considering, musing, hatching— The sea knows Nitti's here, and it knows her state. Along the shore, the black water is forming furrows, and they're advancing toward her. The crests mount as she watches, bases thickening, blades growing sharper.

Will Nitti retreat? Does she have some purpose? No, Kell thinks, no purpose at all. She is bound, rapt by the sight and sound, the water's suggestion, the tireless threats this sea has made. No one—no ayah or lover, housekeeper or friend— knows Nitti better. As cruel as the attachment to Keributan is, it's the strongest one Nitti has.

The waves curl and snap at the strand, rising now to the girl's head. A blade reaches and scrolls, splashing her face, streaking one eye, blacking her nose. Kell wants to take hold, protect her, draw her away. But this isn't his shore, his sky, his sea; he's an observer, viewing Nitti from an impossible distance.

She tries to speak through the slapping waves, then she gasps, turning her head, trying to see through her unblacked eye. A wave drenches her side, spoiling her cheeks, and a child's cry leaves her lips, horror-struck, ooze dripping from her trembling chin.

Kell watches a black wave rise over her crown, cresting, curling and crashing upon her, knocking her legs out, lifting her body and bearing her away.

She's at the mercy of Keributan now, struggling, waving her arms, choking with anguish and foiled hope. Flocks of black petrels leave the sea, roused by the tussle.

Then her limbs grow still. A hoop of black ichor is clamping her chest. Concentered rings circle like iron bands.

All he can see of her now is a head and shoulders bathed in black. Through a shifting lens, she is far and near; he's in and out of her, scanning the shore, feeling the freezing cold, then back in his own head, watching.

All at once the turmoil of Keributan ceases. The muscled black hills, the sweeping ridges— As if heeding some dire command, the great sea grows perfectly still, placid and flat as a mirror.

Nitti's bobbing silhouette is facing the cobbled shore.

She sees the lone tree, bare and bleached, and the giant python coiled on a projecting bough.

The snake's long head is pointed at her, watching. It has waited in that tree for months and years. Moss has grown on its back, gracing its reticulations. Now, as it swings its neck and turns its head, an orange fire flashes in its eye.

Now, right now— The snake begins its descent.

Kell is watching. And so is Nitti.

The coil is unwinding, glittering as if it's covered with oil. The python's hind parts circle the bough, anchoring, and its head starts down. Faceted skin, its scaly neck, winking and winding like a twisted liana, shimmering with blue iridescence. Hanging and turning. Coiling and twisting— For Kell, a familiar image. The python is a helical genome. Its reticulations are windows of doom, the interlocked letters of a code he can't change.

The snake's head touches the cobbles.

The head waits as the giant body collects on the rocky surface around it. Then the head starts forward and, bending and bending, the long body turns into a rippling log, a living pipe possessed by undulations. Moving toward the water, making for Nitti.

Arrow-straight, it enters the quiet black sea; and then it's essing again.

Nitti is watching, seeing it approach.

The python's head is above the water, its long body swimming behind and beneath. Is Nitti thinking of escape? What escape could there be?

The python's head is close. She can see its nose and its nostrils sucking; she can see the dark line on the top of its head, and the red of its eye—curtains hung on either side of the vertical pupil. Its forked tongue snips the air, taking her scent.

Then the serpent's head halts, and the monstrous body gathers around it, crowding in loops, until the python is a tangled mass with its head at the center.

Kell can sense its concentration. Behind the motionless head, the snake is kinking its neck like a thumb cocking a trigger, adding length from behind. Length and strength, muscle and mind—

In a heartbeat the python strikes, its essed neck straightens, its jaws flare like an opening hand, sinking into Nitti's shoulder. She can feel the teeth buried deep, the snake pulling her close, coiling itself around her—binding her trunk, wrapping her legs with its tail.

She's trying to cry out, Kell knows, screaming "Ayah" in her mind, twisting in the terrible grip, struggling against it, clawing at the scaly skin, trying to unbind herself. But the snake isn't going to let go. It's tightening at her every breath, compressing her belly, constricting her chest, rolling her over in Keributan.

Nitti's mind blurs, her thoughts foreshorten. Will her heart burst?

In another reality, Kell was hurrying toward her; his legs churned without touching the ground or moving him forward.

The monster's jaws are opening. Nitti sees a pink flash.

Then darkness closes over her.

Can she feel the fangs dragging across her ears? The snake's jaws are dislocating, coming apart. Its throat expands, skin elastic, stretching to accommodate her, and the terrible swallow grows larger and larger. Fangs clamp her neck. The python is pulling her into its throat, swallowing her headfirst. Cold-blooded, reptilian cold— She can feel the chill. Her chest is crushed. Is there any breath left? Is she still aware?

She is, Kell thinks. She can feel the creeping mucosa sliding over her shoulders. The snake's jaw cradles her chest and its terrible teeth walk down her back, while the muscular throat sends her head deeper. The python is dragging her inside it, tissues stretching around her.

She won't last long, but these moments will be the worst in her life.

The python's gape is enormous now, circling her waist. Nitti feels the hooked teeth on her legs, arms chilled and slicked by the monster's gut, while the rippling fabric slides and stretches and muscles her along.

Then the movement stops.

It's so cold for her, Kell thinks. And so dark. But perhaps she feels safe.

The pain is over, and the struggling. The future's no longer in doubt.

Nitti is a food bulge swamped in serpent juice—the final Keributan.

As Kell watches, the python lifts its head. The dislocated parts duck and shift, brows erecting, snout curved up. Then, as the pieces of its head fit back together, the snake sinks until it's fully submerged.

Kell imagines he's still with Nitti, deep in her psyche, feeling what she feels. A merciful calm. The end of fear. The grace of a long-anticipated surrender.

The python's muscular walls massage her, digesting her slowly. Little by little, she will shrink. Her flesh will dissolve. Her bones will turn to powder.

At the center of Kell's awareness, a cloud of pale moths rises, and with the fluttering cloud goes all of Nitti's fixed impressions, her desperate thoughts, her fleeting desires and her conscious mind.

He wakes slowly, in darkness.

The air is thick and pungent, hard to draw in. Every breath is steeped in the odor of Keributan. The gas of dead creatures chokes him.

Kell leans on one arm and his hand presses into a mattress. He is in Nitti's home, not on the cobbled shore.

He draws himself up and feels for her body, but there are only sheets.

He remembers, through his dream, a knock at the door. A taper flickering. An urgent whisper like steam under pressure. And then, as he sank back into sleep, clapping sandals, shuffling feet like a leafy bough brushing the window.

Kell pulls himself to the bed's edge and draws his pants on. He rises, feels a dizziness and takes deep breaths, clearing it slowly. The hibiscus mask hangs on the wall, that piece of carved wood he'd bought at a market. He slides his feet into his shoes, lifts his shirt and faces the door.

When he opens it and looks out, the corridor lamps are lit.

He enters the passage, pulling his shirt on, listening, hearing nothing at first.

Then, as the dining room comes into view, the sound of steps reaches him. A squeak of bare feet, like frogs at the edge of a seep. The whisk of a nightdress like a hurrying skink. Someone mutters. Is it Prawan?

Kell traverses the dining room. The old house seems claustrophobic. Through the doorway, shadows shift, and as he exits the room and turns the corner, a candle flame wavers ahead, stripes crossing his path like a veinage of roots.

He's reached the hall that leads into the waterside wing. Halfway down it, Prawan and Nitti move in a candle's striated aura—a giant nephila's web stretched on guy lines between spiny rattans. He hears the housekeeper mutter again.

Nitti's movements look mechanical. How conscious is she? Half awake, in a depressed state— His dream suggests ominous things. Kell thinks to shout.

He raises his hand, but he holds his tongue. Despite all that's happened, he understands little; but the dark hall draws him like a legion of ants rolling a black road through the trees. Prawan is escorting Nitti to the door at the end of the hall.

Kell is close enough now to see that Nitti is holding something in her hand—the wind-up monkey drummer. Prawan is clasping the other and speaking, but Kell can't parse her words. From outside comes the sigh of a pre-dawn drizzle. In the jungle, drip-tip leaves are feeding tendrils and vines. Fibrous moss, fungal threads, root hairs and twisting branches all tasting and touching each other.

The two draw closer to Ibu's room. Closer, closer— After crossing a stream, you find a flat rock and scrape the leeches off, but the blood from the bites keeps flowing.

The smell of mold reaches him. The planks are silent here, too damp to creak.

The two women are a few feet from the door. Outside, a giant cricket is sawing its wings.

Prawan halts. Her candle rises, and the door appears like a ghostly tree, a thousand luminous beetles squirming over its bark. She lets go of Nitti's hand and reaches for the knob.

Kell hears the latch click.

The door swings back.

Nitti faces the opening, staring through it. What does she see?

The candlelight trembles like a curtain of water, then Nitti is passing through it. Prawan follows.

Kell's left in the hall, watching the doorway, listening.

Inside the room, a light is switched on. On a window by Kell's elbow, a white-lipped frog clings to the glass with bulbed toes. Nitti is in there now, with the mother who didn't want her. Has Susilo's death weakened her resolve? Does she think she's paying some obligation finally come due? Perhaps she is thinking of him, knowing her history has stood between them.

He takes a step forward, seeing a narrow slice through the doorway. A reflected image: a giant black mantis, broken, on its back with one claw in the air. In a long mirror, a woman in a nightgown black as tar—

"Please, no," Nitti says.

Kell takes another step, and the reflected image expands, a confusion of limbs—an old woman's legs, like a swamp tree with stilts and pegs, propped on a bed.

A whimper: Nitti's voice, weak as a child's. "Ibu," she says.

The black arm is extended, frozen or motioning—Kell can't tell.

He can see Ibu through the open door now, and as he turns from the reflection to face her, an eye flashes cinnamon-gold.

The ceiling is low, the paneling dark. Nitti is standing near the foot of the bed, secured in the housekeeper's arms.

Prawan is conducting her, step by step, closer to her mother.

Nitti seems half asleep, barely willful. "I didn't," she says, shaking her head.

She's objecting, weakly, as if she's being forced to solve some problem she can't comprehend. She's put her mind to it, used all the faculties at her command; but despite the effort, she's failing.

Prawan pays no mind to what Nitti is saying, moving her closer to Ibu with every step.

Kell crosses the threshold and sees Ibu for what she is. Hawk-nosed and hollow-cheeked, crippled and stiff—barely conscious. A faint glimmer lends life to her eyes, while a foundering tongue makes thoughtless sounds. She's senseless, inert, unaware that others have entered the room.

Nitti's still edging forward, jaw budging, lips moving, rehearsing perhaps. They reach the head of the bed and Prawan halts. She reaches her hand out, takes hold of Ibu's hovering claw and draws it closer.

Nitti shrieks, drops her toy and jumps as the claw bumps her chest. Her lids flare, terror blossoms in the youthful eyes and she shudders back, staring at Ibu's limb as if it's covered with fire ants. The mad Prawan has grabbed the frozen cripple. She's stroking Ibu, cooing as if some long-sought reconciliation is underway.

The wind-up monkey drummer is face down on the floor, humped and spasming, striking doubles.

"That's enough." Kell strides forward.

A terrorized Nitti sinks to her knees, eyes glazed.

Kell reaches her, descending beside her with his arm round her back.

"Get out," Prawan snarls.

The housekeeper grapples his shoulders. Kell ignores her, trying to help Nitti up. But her fear is shifting to him. Her lips quiver, her hands shake then crumple to fists, and she beats him back, groaning as if the threats she's facing were authored by him.

"You're not wanted," Prawan shrieks.

And Nitti's eyes, full of alarm, echo her words.

Kell lets go of her and as soon as Prawan sees that, she slides between them, embracing her charge, lifting her up.

Nitti clings to Prawan. "Please, please, please," she whimpers. And between each plea, she flinches and gasps, as if a sharp instrument is being thrust into her.

The older woman strokes her back and murmurs assurances, holding her tightly, vaunting their achievement, speaking as if Ibu, renewed by the visit, is taking her daughter back.

It's nonsense, but not to Nitti.

She hears Prawan's words, and she seems to believe them.

She's younger now. Much younger—an innocent girl with startled eyes—the girl in his dream who was swallowed whole by the python of Keributan.

Kell puts his hands on her shoulders, ready to take her forcibly from Prawan. "We're getting you out of here," he says.

Can she hear him?

"Nitti," Kell says.

"You're not wanted," Prawan roars in his face.

Kell, fixed on Nitti's senseless expression, is speechless.

Prawan straight-arms him back across the threshold, leads Nitti through the doorway and pulls the door closed behind them.

Then she starts back down the hall, holding her charge close.

Kell follows, stunned, wondering at Nitti's state. This strange creature seems to have no will of her own.

He hurries his steps to catch them, moving beside her.

"Come with me," he says. "I'll take care of you."

Nitti's steps slow. She blinks.

The depth in her eyes has vanished.

"Nitti," he says.

She seems not to hear. She rests her cheek on the house-keeper's shoulder, oddly relieved, struck by some newfound freedom, as if she is suddenly aware of how absurd it was to be an adult.

Kell steps ahead of her, turning to face her.

"Look at me," he says.

Nitti meets his gaze, but her eyes are blank. She doesn't know who he is.

They've reached the hall entrance. Kwik is there in his nightshirt.

"We need a doctor," Kell shouts to him.

Prawan speaks in a soft voice, her lips to Nitti's ear. "We're so lucky. 'She's returned.' It's the happiest I've seen your mother in a long time."

Kwik is regarding the three with a puzzled expression.

"The doctor—" Kell pulls his mobile from his pocket.

"It's nothing," Prawan laughs, waving the concern away. And to Nitti, "You don't need the doctor, dear. Do you?"

Nitti shakes her head.

Kwik smiles, reassured.

Kell's fingers are frozen over his phone. Prawan faces him, jowls sagging, aping his disappointment, as if she'd always had his best interests at heart.

"There's nothing left for you here," she says.

He can see Nitti now. The real Nitti. The Nitti behind the mask.

Fear had halted her growth. She'd been frozen in time. Experience couldn't change her, and neither could a man's love, no matter how genuine or innocently offered.

"There's nothing left for you," Prawan says again.

Kell feels the wish in his heart shrinking. Nitti was a stranger to him, and always had been.

Kwik is at his elbow.

"Show Mr. Kell out," Prawan orders the gardener.

Kwik puts his hand on Kell's back.

"I'm not going to leave her," Kell says.

The gardener has grasped his arm, smiling, kindly. His rumpled clothing smells of green clippings. Not like this, Kell thinks. But he's watching the smile and letting himself be guided. Behind him Prawan makes a guttural sound, like an agamid in the undergrowth with an insect in its mouth.

Down the corridor Kwik escorts him, through the dining area, along the hall and into the octagonal guest room.

186

The scent of aquilaria, the low table and chairs—to the right-side door.

Kell pauses on the threshold, breathing the fragrance that masks the fungus and mold. "I'll be back," he mutters.

Then the two men descend the outside stair.

The morning cicadas are whirring. The sun glows through a fog in the east. Kwik crosses the gravel with him till they reach the car.

Kell puts his hand in his pocket, finding his keys and the toy shovel. He returns the toy shovel and uses his keys to open the door.

The gardener is patting his back, smiling his reassurance.

Kell sits in the driver's seat and starts the car.

He draws a breath, rolls down the window, looks at Kwik and steers over the gravel toward the road.

What has happened? he thinks. Heartstruck, helpless—He had run an experiment on behalf of them both. He'd raised their hopes, and he'd seen them cast down.

In the rearview mirror, the jungle appears behind the house. Sounds reach him—a coucal's *twerk*, hornets buzzing, hoppers ticking and the river humming beneath. Love has two faces, he thinks. You could find yourself in someone you love, or could lose yourself. For Nitti, the instinct to lose had been coded.

Then a strange thought strikes him: he'd been her nemesis. He was the python watching from a leafless tree with the letters of a fateful code on his back. His desire for Nitti had allowed Ibu and Keributan to consume her.

187

He accelerates slowly, retreating as he would from a nest of wasps he'd disturbed. The din of the jungle fades, and when Kell looks again in his rearview mirror, the house and the river have disappeared.

Rich Shapero's novels dare readers with giant metaphors, magnificent obsessions and potent ideas. His casts of idealistic lovers, laboring miners, and rebellious artists all rate ideas as paramount, more important than life itself. They traverse wild landscapes and visionary realms, imagining gods who in turn imagine them. Like the seekers themselves, readers grapple with revealing truths about human potential. *Hibiscus Mask* and his previous titles—*Beneath Caaqi's Wings, Dreams of Delphine, The Slide That Buried Rightful, Dissolve, Island Fruit Remedy, Balcony of Fog, Rin, Tongue and Dorner, Arms from the Sea, The Hope We Seek, Too Far,* and *Wild Animus*—are available in hardcover and as ebooks. They also combine music, visual art, animation and video in the TooFar Media app. Shapero spins provocative stories for the eyes, ears, and imagination.